Grandma Got Run Over
By A Demon

Grandma Got Run Over By A Demon

A Ravenmist Whodunit
Book Four

By Olivia Jaymes

www.OliviaJaymes.com

Chapter One

THE DAY AFTER Thanksgiving is a good day for many things. Recovering from a huge meal, perhaps. Or maybe braving the crowds and hitting the mall. Even better might be binge watching a television show that you'd been wanting to see for a long time, or eating leftovers with family and friends.

I wasn't doing any of that.

I was currently standing out in the cold in the center of town yelling at Lloyd Farraday to move a giant Douglas Fir a foot to the left. We were getting ready for the annual play and tree-lighting ceremony on Saturday night. Each year the town held a reenactment of the first Christmas in Ravenmist and it was a big event.

I'll warn you that the production is strictly amateur, the actors and stagehands made up of local teenagers. Elliott Farraday, Lloyd's twin brother and a member of one of the town's founding families, was directing the annual show. He'd been the director for the last ten years and before him it had been his father, Frank.

Before you even ask, yes, I was in the play my junior year in high school but I didn't have a major role. Basically, I was scenery which was in line with my talent level, although I have to say that we were essentially a no-talent bunch that particular year. A rag-tag group of thespians at best. Our most talented guy could play the spoons.

Have you ever heard "Silent Night" played on the spoons? It's epic. Whether that actually happened on the first Christmas in Ravenmist I can't say, but poor Frank Farraday did his best with what he had to work with. Every year there were tweaks and perhaps a bit of creative license. It was kind of fun never knowing what to expect.

"To the left," I called out again, waving my hand in that direction. "About six more inches."

This time Lloyd seemed to get what I was saying and the Douglas Fir was positioned perfectly on the platform. Immediately a group of people from the Moose Lodge scrambled around it like mice on cheddar cheese and began to decorate it, stringing lights and hanging brightly colored glass balls. While the play might change slightly each year, the decorations for the tree didn't vary at all. In fact, I was sure that the same ornaments and garland being hung today had been in use when I was a toddler. They'd seen some wear.

Let's just say that the tree looked its best at night.

Oops. I really should introduce myself, shouldn't I? Where are my manners? My mother would be appalled.

My name is Theodosia "Tedi" Hamilton and I'm the proprietor of the Ravenmist Inn in Ravenmist, Illinois. The inn is a rambling old Victorian that's been in my father's family for generations, consisting of several acres and six restored buildings. I'm also the president of the local paranormal society and I'll answer your question before you even have to ask it.

Yes, ghosts are real. As in *really* real. Big time real.

The whole town of Ravenmist, Illinois is, in fact, crazy haunted. I've spoken to several spirits, including one named Terrence who lives in my closet. But that's a story for another time.

Lloyd jogged up to me, a big grin on his face. "How does it look? I think it looks really good."

"It looks great," I assured him, craning my neck to see the highest branches. It was taller than last year. "Now all we have to do is get the tree decorated."

He nodded in agreement. "I have about a dozen people for the job. We'll be done before you know it."

"Excellent. I'll leave it in your hands then. I need to go check–"

I didn't get any further because Iris Martin flew out of the front doors of the civic center along with her mother, Natalie. The former was calling my name and waving a folder in the air to get my attention.

"Yoo-hoo! Tedi! I have those brochures for you," Iris said, slightly out of breath. The Martins were also one of the founding families of Ravenmist, and Iris was the head of the historical society putting together the holiday display of town artifacts. "I'm glad I caught you."

"By the skin of your teeth. I was headed back to the inn to make sure the decorations were going up there, too."

The decorating would take days and an army of people, but it was a tradition that the Ravenmist Inn looked like Santa's workshop had exploded in it. I took great pride in my holiday spirit.

"I was planning to stop at the inn on our way out of town," Iris explained. "We're heading to Deauville to pick up two lanterns for the display."

My ears perked up. "Something new? That's exciting."

Natalie huffed and shook her head. "Sadly, no. Those Farradays lent the lanterns to their daughter and son-in-law to display in their home in Deauville. Can you imagine? Priceless historical artifacts sitting on a fireplace mantle? It's outrageous. If anything happened—"

"Mother," Iris broke in sharply. "The lanterns belong to the Farraday family. If they want to keep them in their home then they can do that."

Thank goodness Lloyd had ducked away the minute that he saw Natalie and Iris. He didn't have to hear what was being said about his relatives.

Natalie sniffed at the mere suggestion. "The Farradays have never understood the importance of history. But that's just my opinion. I could be wrong."

This might be a good time to mention that although both the Martins and Farradays could claim to be founding families of Ravenmist, they couldn't claim to be friendly. To each other.

There was a little bit of Capulet and Montague going on here and had been for many years.

"Mother," Iris sighed. "You know I hate it when you talk like that. It's not nice."

Natalie Farraday's mouth twisted. "Those Farradays—"

"Are just trying to live their lives in peace," Iris cut in. "Just like we are. They've done nothing to deserve this. You don't even know why you don't like them, do you?"

"I know that I can't believe my daughter is taking their side."

"I'm not taking a side. I'm simply saying that they're human beings, too." Iris turned back to me, slightly flustered. "I'm sorry, Tedi. I think we got sidetracked for a moment."

Iris's mother was a handful on good days so I felt for her. Natalie was known for being that one person that always wanted to "speak to the manager".

"No issue. I do appreciate the brochures. I'll put them out for my guests."

"I hope we get a big turnout this year," Iris replied with a smile. "Is the inn booked up?"

"Completely," I assured her. "I could have filled it three times over so we may have record attendance."

It often surprised me how the casual tourist was interested in our town history or a tree-lighting ceremony, but we'd made something of a reputation on being quaint...and haunted.

"Iris, where else do we need to drop off the brochures?" Natalie asked, checking her watch and sighing loudly. "We need to get on the road soon."

"Just Daisy's," Iris said, biting her lip. "Tedi, I don't suppose–"

"I can do that," I said, accepting another stack of paper. "I'm going right by there."

I bid them goodbye, along with Lloyd, who had made excellent progress on decorating the tree, and headed to Daisy's. The day was sunny and cold and there was a little spring in my step as I walked. There was just something about this time of year that made me happy. Maybe it was the lights or the music or all that goodwill toward men but I was a complete sucker for it.

Daisy wasn't at the diner she owned as she'd taken the morning off after a busy Thanksgiving Day, so I left the historical society brochures with her second-in-command and headed back to the inn. Despite eating a metric ton of food the day before, I was starving for lunch. When I pushed open the front door of the inn, my nostrils were assailed with the delicious smell of today's chef's special – parmesan crusted chicken breast. My stomach gurgled in anticipation and I made a beeline for the kitchen, waving at Tina who was manning the desk today. I made it no farther, however, as she waved me back with an apologetic smile.

"Hey Tina, what's up? Is there a problem?"

Tina rarely had issues. She'd worked at the inn on and off for years while completing her degree in business.

"It's not really a problem per se…"

Oookay….then what was it?

She looked so unsure, which wasn't her usual expression at

all. She was confident and bouncy even at the worst of times. Maybe she was having issues with her boyfriend and needed to take the rest of the day off.

"Why don't you tell me about it?" I encouraged. "It can't be all that bad."

"We have new guests."

That didn't sound that ominous. We were an inn, after all.

"Was there a problem with their reservation?"

Tina shook her head, and then cast a quick glance over her shoulder and toward the dining room. "No, that was fine. It's...them."

"Them?"

"Arthur and Belinda Cambridge. They're in the Blackwood Suite."

The Blackwood Suite was our nicest accommodation. A two-bedroom with a large bathroom that boasted a jetted tub and walk-in shower. It was often used for honeymoons and such.

"And they don't like it?"

I was beginning to become impatient with our game of Twenty Questions. What the flip was wrong with these guests?

Raised voices from the dining room interrupted whatever Tina might have replied. My intuition told me that whatever was making a racket in my dining room was what Tina had been trying to tell me about. Couldn't we get through one holiday without a dust up?

"I'm going to see what's going on in the dining room. Am I going to find out the problem you're telling me about when I get there?"

Eyes wide, Tina nodded. It was my managerial duty to deal with it so I hurried into the dining room to find Frank Farraday, father to Elliott and Lloyd, having a loud argument with an older, well-dressed man. They were red-faced and waving pointed fingers so it looked like it might get nasty. I couldn't imagine what was upsetting Frank, who was as mild-mannered as could be. I'd never even heard him raise his voice my entire life.

Until today.

I was about to tell them to quiet down and take it someplace else but an even larger figure cut in front of me and placed himself right in between the two men.

"Is there a problem here?"

Jack. Our town sheriff.

Did he have some sort of radar? He was always Johnny-on-the-spot.

No one spoke, which seemed to irritate Jack. It didn't take much these days. He'd been like a bear with a sore paw for months. Since summer, to be exact.

"Well?" he prompted. "Is anyone going to answer my question?"

Finally, Frank shrugged and crossed his arms over his chest. "This…person is Arthur Cambridge and his daughter Belinda. Apparently, they're interested in buying the Farraday family diaries. Which are not for sale. Ever. And that's final."

I hadn't even noticed the younger woman who was standing

a few feet away. If you concentrated real hard, you could smell the money from ten paces.

Suddenly I felt decidedly under-dressed in my worn blue jeans and black sweater. I'd dressed for warmth and comfort this morning, but the female that stood in my dining room clearly didn't share that idea. Wearing a sapphire blue dress and a strand of pearls, she teetered on high heels that would have sent me to the hospital with a broken ankle. I had to admire her ability to balance on the tiniest pinpoint. She could have walked a high wire for a living.

The older man was dressed in a dark business suit with a grey wool coat over the top, and his shoes were shined to perfection, almost as glittery as the gold and diamond watch on his wrist.

"Everyone has their price," Arthur Cambridge snarled. "I just haven't found it yet."

Frank harrumphed and shook his head. "Once and for all, they're not for sale. Not for any price. I don't want to discuss it. They're not for sale. Period."

"If we could just talk–"

Frank threw up his hands in disgust. "I don't want to talk to you. Go away!"

Jack took a step toward Arthur Cambridge, crowding him so he had to move back. "Okay, that's fine, Frank. No one is going to force you to sell them or even discuss it. Now, Mr. Cambridge, it appears that the item in question isn't for sale."

"Come on, Dad," the daughter urged, tugging at her father's sleeve. "Let's go."

"That's good advice," Jack said with a nod. "I'd take it, if I were you."

"I'll be back," Cambridge said as his daughter pushed him out of the dining room and into the lobby. "This isn't over."

"Thanks for the warning, man," Frank groaned, rubbing at the back of his neck. "Thanks, Sheriff. I don't know who that guy is but I don't have any interest in talking to him."

"No problem," Jack said. "Let me know if he bothers you again."

"Believe me, I will." Frank nodded at me. "Sorry about that. I swear I didn't start it."

"I believe you, but just so that you know, Arthur Cambridge and his daughter have checked into the inn. I have a feeling he isn't going to give up."

"Yes, he will," Jack growled. "Or I'll personally check him out of his room and escort him to the city line."

Frank chuckled and headed toward the back door. "We can always count on you, Sheriff, to have our backs. Now if you'll excuse me, I have to check in with Elliott at the civic center."

Now I was standing with Jack in my dining room. I hadn't had near enough caffeine to deal with him today. Honestly, I was getting tired of his attitude. I wasn't the enemy and neither was the town. If he didn't like living in a rural area then maybe he should pack up and go back to Chicago. He needed a good talking-to and I wasn't above giving it to him. Someone needed to do it.

"Jack."

"Tedi."

"We need to talk."

"Okay. Talk."

"In private," I hissed, motioning for him to follow me into the kitchen. We'd had some of our best conversations in that loud and busy space. He settled in at the counter while I filled two coffee cups. Mostly for me. I had no idea if he needed it but I didn't want to be rude.

Well...that wasn't actually true. I kind of wanted to be rude to Jack right now. I sat next to him and sipped at the dark brew.

"First of all, thank you for intervening there. It was getting rather heated."

"Just doing my job."

"Right. Your job. Anyhoo, let's talk about that. Lately, you've been doing your job in sort of a way...well...what I'm trying to say is..."

Jack leaned down until we were almost nose to nose.

"What are you trying to say? You usually don't have any trouble talking to me."

That wasn't always the case.

I huffed out a breath and lifted my chin. He was going to argue with me but I was ready. With examples. I had receipts, people.

"Fine. You've been rather...*surly* lately. Are you aware of that?"

I thought he'd take offense but instead he simply smiled.

He *smiled*. What was that about?

"I am, Tedi, and I don't think it's a problem."

"For you. But what about all of the innocent people around you?"

Jack barked with laughter. "Innocent? That's rich. They'll adjust."

This wasn't in the least funny.

"So is this permanent? Your bad mood, I mean? I'm asking for a friend."

"I'm not in a bad mood. This is my sparkling personality." His radio crackled to life, reminding us both that he was on duty. "I have to go. We can talk about this another time."

"Fine."

"If Arthur Cambridge causes any more trouble let me know."

"I will."

"I have to go, Tedi."

For a moment, Jack seemed to hesitate but it was only a split second and then he was gone. I blew out a relieved breath and sat back down at the counter with my coffee. Something was going on with Jack Garrett and I didn't have a clue as to what it was or how to fix it. He was just one more mystery in this town and frankly, I didn't need another one. My plate was full. Did I mention our demon problem?

Now to add to it, Jack was being the devil.

I didn't have the patience for it. He could be as nasty as he wanted to be. I'd tried to talk to him, but I was pretty busy these days trying to keep Ravenmist from being slaughtered in an apocalypse. His piddly problems would have to wait.

Chapter Two

I HAD BIGGER issues at hand than Jack's lousy attitude, which is why I was sitting in my friend Missy's bookstore discussing the latest news from her family. Missy is a Grim Reaper – or a better description might be a Grim Reaper Helper – and that means that her relatives are all supernatural beings. If anyone would be able to shed light on our good versus evil, demons living in Ravenmist problem, then it would be Missy's family.

"There isn't any news. Grandma said she's looked through all of her books and can't find anything. She's tried to contact some old friends but so far she hasn't had any luck."

Missy and I had been hitting walls every which way we turned in the last several months. Since we'd found out that Ravenmist might be ground zero for an epic battle between good and evil we'd been doing everything in our power to find out just who the demon was that had come to town. He or she had brought mammoth amounts of supernatural energy with them and now all the spirits living in our town were practically alive. They only lacked a pulse and respiration, and for all we knew that could be next.

"Old friends?" I echoed. "As in supernatural friends? Like vampires, werewolves, and voodoo priestesses?"

Missy rolled her eyes. "I don't think vampires and were-wolves are real, Tedi. And as for voodoo...don't mess with it."

"So voodoo is real, but the Easter Bunny isn't?"

"Just leave it alone. In fact, stay away from Ouija boards, too."

"If I want to talk to the dead, I'll talk to Terrence. Or Amelia and Charles."

With a cold breeze and a pop, Edward appeared next to Missy, holding a stack of books. He was the "ghost in residence" here at the bookshop.

"What am I, chopped liver?" he asked with a scowl. "You can talk to me, too."

The last thing I needed was a spirit upset with me.

"Of course, I can," I replied in a soothing tone. "Because I didn't see you, I wasn't even sure you were here today. I thought you and Terrence might be working together."

Terrence is my ghost in residence at the inn, the one I mentioned earlier. He and Edward were finishing up a documentary about the lives of ghosts and planning to upload it to YouTube very soon. So far, I'd managed to find all sorts of topics they needed to cover in the documentary, but I was running out of ideas and the day that they would finish was coming soon.

Edward shrugged. "I don't know what Terrence is doing today, but I'm working. I have a job here now."

And with another pop, he was gone.

Heavens to Betsy, say it wasn't so. Missy hadn't given in, had she? Edward and Terrence had been bugging us for employment for the last several weeks. They wanted to earn money.

What in the world is a ghost going to do with money?

I'm so glad you asked.

Terrence told me that he wanted to buy a car because he missed driving. Edward wanted to buy a new, more powerful laptop. Personally, I found it disturbing that the spirits in Ravenmist were turning to consumerism, especially at this time of year.

I gave Missy an accusing stare. "You didn't."

She shifted uncomfortably in her chair. "Lonnie had to cut back on his hours and I needed the help. Edward is only working about ten hours a week. I have him tidy up and keep the bookshelves clean."

Rubbing at my now throbbing temples, I shook my head. "Now Terrence is going to be on my case constantly. Just how are you paying Edward, anyway? He doesn't have a social security number."

"Cash under the table," Missy sighed. "I did ask him about a social security number but if he had one, he doesn't remember it."

"I hope the IRS doesn't find out."

Missy's brows rose. "If the IRS finds out I'm paying a ghost cash under the table then we have some serious issues."

I had to ask.

"How's Edward working out?"

"He's doing a good job. He's very conscientious. I could do much worse." She sighed again. "I'm sorry if I've put you in a difficult position."

"It's fine. I'll just have to find something that Terrence can do that doesn't have much interaction with the public."

"Maybe he can do some of your paperwork?" Missy suggested. "He's good on the computer."

I'd been trying to offload the inventorying for years but hadn't found anyone who could do a decent job. Maybe...

"So have you mailed your letter to Santa yet?" Missy asked. "I did this morning."

Ravenmist had always had a thing about everyone mailing a letter to Santa and as I'd grown older, I'd thought it was a cute and lovely little custom that helped everyone get in the spirit of the season. Now that I knew Santa Claus was real – Missy had told me – it brought a whole new meaning to writing a letter.

"I need to work on it. My goal is to mail it tomorrow." I paused for a moment but then plunged in. Missy and I didn't have any secrets from one another. Heck, we were hunting demons together. "So...what did you ask for?"

"The usual. Peace on earth, goodwill toward men," she said with a smirk. "And chocolate. Lots of chocolate."

"That's it?"

She and I had a long tradition of crazy Christmas lists. One year I'd asked for a pony.

I didn't get it, of course. But I'd asked.

Because you can't win if you don't play. Am I right, people?

"Well...I might have added a bottle of that expensive perfume that I love so much."

"And?"

"Dinner at Chez Henri in the city."

Chez Henri was Missy's absolute favorite place to eat in the entire world. Her parents had taken her there on her sixteenth birthday and an obsession had been born. She'd been there nine times so far.

"I don't know about Santa but I'm guessing that Dylan could handle those requests."

Dylan and Missy had been boyfriend and girlfriend for...forever. Okay, maybe not that long, but long enough that he knew what would make her over the moon for Christmas.

"He could. What are you going to ask for?"

That was a good question. There wasn't much that I needed. As a grown woman with a regular income, if there was something that I wanted and it wasn't prohibitively expensive, I could buy it for myself. I didn't need Santa for that, although I wouldn't say no to a pony.

"I was thinking of asking Santa for the name of the demon."

There. I'd said it.

Missy's eyes widened. "Santa? That's...bold."

"I don't need new socks. I need to know who the demon is and so far, we've had zero luck figuring that out. It's a shot in the dark but at this point I'm not sure we have anything to lose."

"I didn't even think about asking Santa about the demon. I mean...that's not something that the elves can whip up in the factory."

"The elves are real, too? You never mentioned that."

Missy gave me a look that said I should have known it.

"So do you think I'm crazy for asking? We're at the end of our rope."

Missy didn't answer right away, clearly gathering her thoughts.

"I know that we've talked about finding the demon and all of that but at some point, I think we both have to trust that this person knows what he's doing. The battle between good and evil has been going on long before we were born and will probably be going on after we're gone. We're just small cogs in the wheel, Tedi. Does the demon even need us? Maybe he's got this handled, and we're worrying over nothing."

Missy was far more of an optimist than I would ever be, no matter how hard I tried.

"We don't know anything for sure. But wouldn't you feel more secure if we knew who the demon was and we could talk to he or she?"

"I do want to know. I'm just not sure that we're ever going to find out, that's all."

I'd already made my decision. It couldn't hurt to ask.

"I'm going to put it on my list," I finally said. "With my history of not getting what I want on Christmas morning, I'm probably just wasting my time anyway."

"Maybe if you weren't always on the naughty list..." Missy giggled. "Have you been a good girl this year?"

I'd been a freakin' angel.

And frankly, it hadn't been easy. The alternatives were always so much fun.

LATER THAT EVENING when I was reclining on the couch, the television humming softly in the background, I took pen to paper. It was time to write my letter.

I started out as I usually did. Greeting Santa and asking after his health and that of Mrs. Claus. They weren't as young as they used to be, after all. Then I asked about the elves – now that I knew that they were real – and hoped they were doing okay, too. Finally, I inquired about the reindeer and hoped that they weren't playing any games where others might not feel welcome or included.

Then it was down to the real business of my Christmas list.

Should I just zing in with the big guns and ask about the demon's identity? Or maybe work up to it? Santa might not be able to tell me who the demon was. He was a supernatural being but that didn't mean he would know everyone and everything.

Although I kind of felt that he should. He supposedly could see me when I was sleeping…blah blah blah.

"What are you doing, Tedi?"

Terrence. My closet ghost. He was standing – hovering, actually – in between me and the television. He was an avid movie watcher and I was surprised that he wasn't watching the television right now. It's where he spent a great deal of time. I barely remembered my life before Terrence was in it. He was like the brother that I'd never had.

"Writing my letter to Santa. How about you?"

"I was visiting Edward." There was a long pause before he continued. "He has a job with Missy now."

"I heard."

"I asked Missy if she had any other openings but she said that she doesn't."

"Edward is only working a few hours a week."

"Still…he has a job. He has a place to be every day."

Sighing, I placed my paper and pen on the coffee table. "You have a place to be every day too, Terrence."

"It's not the same. Missy needs Edward."

"No," I admitted. "It's not, but that doesn't mean that you aren't important. We need you around here just as much."

"There's so much I could do," he replied, eagerness in his tone. "I could help if you'd only let me."

I'd known this was coming even before I'd talked to Missy today.

"Let me think on it. I'm sure I can find something for you to do."

Terrence did a ghostly fist pump into the air. "Yes. Thank you, Tedi. You won't regret it."

Famous last words. I had a feeling I absolutely would come to regret it but I couldn't keep saying no. Honestly? I'm a pushover. Shhh…don't let out my secret.

"I'm going to go tell Edward. He thinks he's so special because he has a job."

With a whoosh of cool air Terrence was gone, leaving me alone once again. I picked up the paper and pen, determined to finish my letter. I'd think about what job Terrence could do tomorrow.

Tapping the end of my pen against my lips, I decided to start small. Work up to that big request. If Santa couldn't tell me who the demon was, then giving him a few easy ones might be the way to go. Let's see...

That seafoam green sweater in the window at Simpson's. It was pretty, not too expensive, and it would look amazing on me. Size medium.

Hmmm....how about a complete set of *Little House* books. I'd been a Laura Ingalls Wilder fanatic since childhood and was the proud owner of all of her books, but sadly a roof leak had ruined them and several Harry Potter editions. I'd been meaning to mention it to Missy but hadn't had a chance yet.

And that red lipstick I'd seen at the cosmetic counter a few weeks ago. Crimson velvet. I didn't need any more lipstick but I wanted it.

Snow. I wanted it to snow, too. In this part of Illinois it wasn't common to have snow early in December, and according to the weatherman he didn't think we would be getting it anytime soon. Surely Santa could conjure up some snowflakes?

A wish on a shooting star.

I'd heard stories but I'd never actually seen one. I'd wish for the whole Armageddon thing to go away and not come back.

I needed to ask for something that really wasn't for me. How about...an end to the feud between the Martins and Farradays? That had been going on for generations but surely the whole town would be better off if they weren't arguing with one another.

And last, but surely not least...to know the identity of the demon. It was a great deal to ask of St. Nick but if anyone could do it, he could. I just hoped he was up to the task.

There was no way that I was on the naughty list this year. I'd been good and could prove it if I needed to. Was there some sort of court for this? Did I need a lawyer?

Feeling satisfied, I sealed up the letter and placed it on the kitchen counter. I'd mail it first thing in the morning.

It was easily the most important letter I'd ever written to Santa Claus.

Chapter Three

B RIGHT AND EARLY the next day, I headed out into the chilly morning to mail my letter to Santa. In Ravenmist there was only one mailbox that would accept letters to Santa, and it was located right by the civic center and the Christmas tree.

Lloyd and his crew had done their magic. The tree was fully decorated and ready for the lighting ceremony tonight. I might not be a child any longer but that didn't stop me from being ridiculously excited about the upcoming events. The play and the tree-lighting were some of my favorite holiday traditions.

I marched up to the mailbox, opened the lid, took a deep breath, and then slid the letter in the slot. Done. Within hours, it would be on its way to Santa.

A large hand came to rest on top of the mailbox. Jack. And his teenage son Tyler, too.

"Jack."

"Tedi."

"You're out and about early on a Saturday morning."

"Tyler and I are going to Daisy's for breakfast. Care to join us?"

Normally I would never say no to eating breakfast at Daisy's. It was, in fact, my planned next stop but the thought of eating with Jack had me hesitating. He hadn't exactly been great company lately.

"I'd love to hear more about the first Christmas in Ravenmist," Tyler piped up. "I only know what we're doing in the play."

I couldn't turn down the opportunity to educate an eager young man about the history of our fine town. So that's how I ended up sitting across from Jack and Tyler at The Grateful Raven. We ordered and then Tyler saw a friend across the room and was immediately gone, leaving Jack and myself alone.

Oh goody.

He seemed content to not speak and simply sip his coffee, but after a few minutes I couldn't take the silence.

"What part does Tyler have in the play?"

"He's one of the settlers. He doesn't have any lines."

Scenery. Just like me.

"Those are very important roles, Jack. They add an authenticity to the play that wouldn't be there otherwise."

So I'd been told by Frank Farraday.

"I'm sure it is. I guess this means that I have to watch it this year."

"You didn't see the play last year?"

It was a huge town event. How did Jack manage to weasel out of it? And how did I not notice that he wasn't there last year?

Right…champagne.

"I was on duty."

It sounded like a perfectly good reason except that Jack's expression was so smug and patronizing I couldn't believe him for even a split second.

"Liar."

His eyes widened comically. "Are you calling me a liar, Tedi Hamilton? That's cruel."

Snorting, I rolled my eyes. "You have the skin of a rhinoceros. Nothing bothers you. Now, seriously. What do you think of the tree placement? Right smack dab in the center, am I right?"

Crossing his arms, Jack nodded in agreement. "Tree placement? Ten out of ten. Tree decorations? Two out of ten. What's going on here? Do we need to take up a collection or something? Sell some brownies? Those are the saddest looking decorations I've ever seen. They're pathetic."

He was right but he didn't understand.

"They're a tradition."

His brows rose. "It's a tradition for the town tree to look awful?"

He just didn't get it. He hated traditions.

"The decorations are older than me."

"And they look it."

"Can you keep your voice down? You don't want others to hear you."

"Why? People can't handle the truth? The decorations have seen better days. About twenty years ago. If the town can't afford it, I'll buy them myself and make it a gift."

I threw up my hands in frustration. Talking to this man was like talking to a wall.

"It's not about the decorations. It's about the tradition."

"Let me know when the town is tired of tradition. I'll write a check."

This was how most of our conversation were going these days. He'd been assimilating so well into small town life and then…bam! He'd gone off to Chicago for a few weeks over the summer and he'd come back different. More like the man that he'd been when he first moved to Ravenmist.

A couple of steps forward and a bunch of steps back.

At this point, you're probably wondering about my date with Jack since he'd asked me last May. I'm happy to bring you up to date on that.

It didn't happen. At all.

He'd asked and I'd said yes. We'd sort of planned it for when Tyler spent time in Chicago with his mother, but then something happened that I'm still not clear on. Tyler was only with his mom about a week when Jack shot out of town unexpectedly with hardly a word to anyone except that he was going to Chicago. Apparently, Tyler had called and Jack was on the road a few hours later. Jack ended up taking his vacation time and staying a few weeks. When he came back, he was grumbling and growly and generally not much fun to be around. He never mentioned our date again and neither did I.

What was I going to say? *Hey, Jack don't you want to date me anymore?* That sounded far too needy.

And I wasn't needy. I was just fine on my own, thank you very much.

"So what was in your letter to Santa?"

"How do you know that it was a letter to Santa?"

Chuckling, Jack just grinned. "Let's just call it a gut feeling. So what did you ask for?"

"It's really none of your business," I replied tartly. "Did you write a letter to Santa?"

"No, I'm on the permanent naughty list."

I could see how that would happen.

"But if you weren't, what would you ask for?"

For some reason, I really wanted to know.

He shrugged. "The usual. Peace on earth and goodwill toward men."

"Only men? Not women, too?"

"How about goodwill toward humanity? I'm an equal opportunity kind of guy."

"That sounds a little more…twenty-first century."

"How was your Thanksgiving?"

Did he really care? I'd invited him and Tyler but he'd said they were *busy*.

"It was good. My dad was there and Missy and Dylan came by for dessert. We were their third stop of the day so they were pretty full by the time they got to us. How about you?"

"Tyler and I volunteered to help Daisy yesterday."

Daisy always opened up the diner for the homeless or anyone who might be alone on Thanksgiving. I had to admit that I was surprised to hear that Jack and his son had spent the day there.

"That's…wonderful. She can always use more hands."

"That's what I thought. Plus, Tyler needed volunteer hours for school." He took another sip of coffee. "Has Arthur Cambridge been causing any more trouble?"

I'd seen Mr. Cambridge and his daughter in the dining room this morning, but they'd been heads down talking to one another and didn't seem to be bothering anyone else.

"No, but I'm keeping an eye on them. Their reservation is through the weekend."

They were scheduled to check out Monday morning.

Jack glanced over to where Tyler was chatting with a friend. "What are these artifacts that Cambridge is interested in buying? What makes them valuable?"

"They're really only valuable to someone who is interested in history. There are some dishes, a few pieces of furniture, a painting, some books, and of course the set of diaries of Becky Farraday. Becky was a young wife and mother when her husband and his family moved to Ravenmist to make a new life. She'd kept meticulous records of those first few years and she was the lone reason current residents know about the first Christmas."

"You've read the diaries?"

"Back then we had to for school. I guess they don't have the kids do that anymore. Actually, I really enjoyed reading them. There are a lot of boring parts where she talks about crops and weather but some of it is really fascinating." I gave Jack a playful smile. "There's a legend that somewhere in the diaries is the location of the money that the Farradays brought with them to Ravenmist. It's supposedly in some sort of code, but no one really believes it."

For some reason Jack thought that was hilarious. His shoulders shook with laughter and his cheeks turned red. "You're telling me that this town believes in ghosts and Santa Claus but a treasure map is simply too far-fetched? Interesting."

Desperately needing the caffeine, I signaled the waitress for more coffee. "So Cambridge might want the artifacts for themselves and their historical value or he might want them for the treasure. But either way it doesn't matter because the Farraday family isn't going to sell them. They'd never do that."

"That's not what Natalie Martin thinks."

Sighing, I shook my head. "That's a whole other story."

Jack leaned forward, his elbows resting on the table between us. "Help me understand this situation between the Farradays and the Martins. I get that they don't like each other, but I don't understand why."

"They don't really understand why," I replied with a sigh. "It's sort of a long story and it goes way back to the beginning of Ravenmist. The Martins and the Farradays were two of the three founding families. The third died out many years ago. Anyway, they were all good friends and helped build the town together. I don't have all the details because at this point it's all just hearsay, but supposedly there was a falling out between the two patriarchs. Farraday thought that Martin was stealing from him, and Martin thought that Farraday was stealing from him. Neither could prove anything but it didn't stop the accusations."

"So they're feuding?"

"Not really. They just try to pretend the other family doesn't exist. We're Midwesterners, Jack. We don't feud. We dysfunctionally ignore the situation as long as possible."

"It sounds passive-aggressive."

"It is, but it works for us most of the time. Things get a little tense this time of the year because the town founding story is out there for everyone to see in the play. Only the good stuff, of course."

"We can't air the dirty laundry for the tourists," Jack mocked as their plates were slid in front of them. He'd ordered the full platter with eggs, bacon, hash browns, toast, and a fresh baked cinnamon roll. I'd ordered the blueberry pancakes and had already decided that he wasn't getting a bite no matter how much he begged. Jack loved blueberries but for some reason he never ordered them.

"Once again, we're stoic Midwesterners. We don't go on and on about our interpersonal problems. How are your eggs?"

"Excellent." Jack waved to Tyler who reluctantly left his friend to come eat. He'd ordered the waffles. "Can I try a bite of your pancakes? They look good."

He had some nerve asking when he'd been such a grouchy-pants these last months.

I held up my fork in a warning manner. "One bite. You don't want to be on the wrong side of these tines."

It was only one bite.

And it was the season of *giving*.

Chapter Four

A FTER BREAKFAST I returned to the inn determined to sneak into my office and work on those planning spreadsheets for next year that I'd been putting off. It wouldn't take more than a few hours, but I'd been so busy with Thanksgiving dinner that I'd pushed it out of my mind until I could better concentrate on it.

The time had come. I was in between holidays and my schedule wasn't going to get any better in the near future. I grabbed a cup of coffee and ducked into my office, closing the door behind me as if to shut out the rest of the world. Two hours later I stumbled out, a bit groggy and wondering what day, month, and year it was.

"Pumpkin? Are you okay?"

I blinked a few times and my vision cleared, revealing my father standing there holding a wreath and wearing a concerned expression.

"Spreadsheets," I croaked, dramatically holding onto the doorframe. Where was that fainting couch when I needed it? "Need coffee."

Chuckling, he set the wreath down on a side table and linked our arms together to lead me into the kitchen. "Then we need to get you that coffee right away. Are you done with your work?"

"I am. For now, anyway. How's the decorating going?"

Every year my father helped decorate the inn for the holidays. He'd done it before I took over and all the way back to when he was a boy. For him it was a tradition. One I was extremely grateful for.

He poured us two mugs of steaming hot coffee and we sat down in the mostly empty dining room. "It's going okay. Some of the garland needs to be replaced along with several light strings. They don't make them like they used to. We used your grandmother's light strings for more than a decade. These days I'm lucky to get a couple of seasons out of them."

My dad loved to complain about the way things were made now. He and I could bond over that because I agreed and I wasn't even forty yet.

My gaze wandered around the large dining room. "What you've done looks amazing so far. What do you have left?"

"The stairwells and then we need to finish the outside. We should be done by Monday or Tuesday, barring bad weather."

"It's supposed to be sunny."

The sound of raised voices interrupted whatever would have been my dad's reply. In the far corner of the dining room Belinda Cambridge was arguing loudly with the hostess and wildly gesticulating with her hands. This couldn't be good.

"Excuse me, Dad."

I was out of my chair and across the room in two seconds. I swear it's my life's work to get in between arguing people. Perhaps I should apply for a job as a deputy on Jack's police force. I had experience.

"Can I help here?"

Belinda Cambridge looked up at me and blinked owlishly. "Who are you?"

"I'm the owner of the inn. Can I help you, Ms. Cambridge?"

Lena, the dining room hostess, was holding a menu in front of her chest as if it was a suit of armor. Her cheeks were flushed and she was breathing hard like she'd just finished a marathon. Normally she was as calm as the Ravenmist Lake.

"You certainly can. First, you can fire this woman here. She was rude to me. Then you can tell her that I need to order a dinner buffet for a hundred for six this evening."

My brain couldn't quite take in all the words that Belinda had used. It sounded like she wanted me to fire Lena and make dinner for a hundred people by six this evening. It was already after eleven.

"Lena, why don't you see if there's anything they need in the kitchen."

Lena didn't have any business in the kitchen and there was nothing they needed, but she took the obvious opportunity to flee and immediately disappeared.

Leaving me and Ms. Cambridge alone. Lucky me.

"Ms. Cambridge, why don't we sit down?"

"I don't want to sit down."

Okey-dokey. We were going to do this standing. I was fine with it.

Belinda Cambridge's gaze ran me up and down. "Are you going to write down my order?"

I'd learned a long time ago not to let people push me around. No matter how much money they had.

"No. No, I'm not. Because there's no way we could cater a hundred people on such short notice. My kitchen already has a full schedule with the play and tree-lighting ceremony tonight."

Her eyes widened as if she'd never heard the word no before. For all I knew, maybe she hadn't.

"Do you know who I am?" Sighing, I had to struggle not to roll my eyes. "My father is a very important man and when he finds out–"

I nodded impatiently. "Right. Yes. I'll be ruined. He knows important people. No one will ever stay here ever again. I'll be living in a box down by the river. Is that what you wanted to say?"

The other woman frowned. "Well…yes."

I shrugged because it was just another day as an innkeeper. "I've heard worse, actually. I'm afraid that we won't be able to accommodate your request to have a buffet for one hundred people by six this evening. Will there be anything else?"

Belinda Cambridge bristled visibly, her chin lifted in defiance. "You haven't heard the last of this. I'll be telling my father right away."

I had no doubt about that.

"If he has any issues, I'll be happy to explain the situation to him as well."

I'd barely finished my sentence when she turned on her precariously high heel and marched out of my dining room. She had a head full of steam and I had a feeling I'd be getting a visit from her father very soon.

"She didn't look very happy, Pumpkin."

My father had wandered over and was watching Belinda Cambridge stomp across the lobby to the elevator.

"She's definitely not happy, Dad. She wanted a buffet for a hundred people by six tonight. I nipped that idea in the bud immediately."

My father's shoulders shook with laughter and his cheeks turned red. "She wanted what? That's crazy. We have a festival tonight to get ready for."

"That's what I told her. Then she asked me if I knew who she was."

My father's brows pinched together. "Is she famous or something? Is she one of those social media stars?"

"No, but apparently her daddy is rich. He's going to come down in here in about five minutes and threaten to ruin my business and life."

"You know, Pumpkin, you might want to watch out for that woman and her father. They look like trouble to me."

My dad was a wise man. In a perfect world I'd give Arthur and Belinda Cambridge a wide berth, but I had a feeling that I wouldn't be given the chance.

THERE WASN'T AN empty seat in the civic center that night for the play recreating the first Christmas in Ravenmist, and I should know. Jack was sitting next to me. Third row from the front. I had sat on the aisle and somehow no one had sat next to me, which in itself was strange. It was always standing room only every year so there shouldn't have been a seat left when Jack showed up two minutes before curtain time. Was the town matchmaking again?

The play went off without a hitch and I had to admit that Jack appeared to be a proud father when Tyler and the rest of the cast took their final bow. The audience gave them a standing ovation which was a heck of a lot more than I got years ago, but this group was far and away more talented. Heck, they'd *sang* "Silent Night" and let me tell you…that's far superior to hearing it on the spoons.

"Tyler did an excellent job."

Jack grinned and nodded. "He sure did. I was surprised that he even wanted to be in the play but he did great. I had no idea that he had an interest in the theatre. He's joined the drama club at school."

I raised my eyebrows comically and jerked my head toward where Tyler was talking to a pretty teenage girl who had played Becky Farraday. "I think I might know why he has a sudden interest."

Jack frowned for a moment and then his expression cleared.

"I guess there are worse reasons to join the drama club. I played football because of pretty girls so this isn't much different."

"Her name is Ellie Travis and she's quite smart. Honor roll. Wants to attend Stanford and be a doctor. She's in the drama club and volunteers at the retirement home once a week after school. Her dad is a financial planner."

More specifically, he was *my* financial planner.

"Maybe she'll light a fire under Tyler and he'll try a little harder in school."

"Love is a powerful force."

Jack's smile was mocking. "It can make a fool out of you, that's for sure."

The audience trickled out to the town square where the tree was waiting to be lit. Jack and I didn't say much as we slowly exited the building. I was supposed to meet Missy out here but I couldn't find her anywhere in the crowd.

We gathered around the tree, the crowd jostling for a good spot to watch the lighting ceremony. Lloyd was manning the electrical cords and his father Frank was pacing back and forth waiting for everyone to get settled. The tree-lighting ceremony started precisely at nine o'clock.

Leaning down, Jack nudged me. "Isn't that Arthur Cambridge and his daughter Belinda?"

Following his gaze, there were the Cambridges standing next to Natalie Martin and having an animated conversation. Were they trying to get her to sell them one of their artifacts?

"I'm trying to stay away from them," I whispered. "I had

words with both today and they think I'm slime."

Jack's brows shot up. "Slime? That's harsh. What was your transgression?"

"I couldn't have the kitchen whip up a buffet for a hundred by six this evening. They were quite unhappy with me and Arthur threatened to tell all of his rich and important friends how uncooperative and unprofessional I've been."

"And what did you tell Arthur?"

"That next time he needed to make those sort of arrangements ahead of time."

"I'm guessing that didn't go over well."

"Like the proverbial lead balloon."

Frank hopped up on the dais and tapped the microphone, sending an ear-splitting squeal across the crowd that was like nails on a chalkboard. Everyone stopped talking though, so it worked.

"Um…excuse me," he said, waving an arm in the air.

The only thing that I could hear was some trees rustling in the breeze.

"Okay, so we're going to get started," he went on. "Every year we light the Ravenmist Christmas tree to kick off the holiday season. For those that have never been to a tree-lighting ceremony, there is a light on the tree for every resident of Ravenmist. This year there are two more lights than last year. We're excited to see the continued growth of our small community."

Frank cleared his throat. "Many years ago, my family, along

with two others, founded this town as a place to belong, a place to put down roots. They wanted their neighbors to feel like family and I think, even all these years later, that we've accomplished that. Now it's time to kick off the holiday season. Lloyd, will you do the honors, please?"

Holding an electrical cord in each hand, Lloyd gave his father a grin before connecting them together. The lights on the tree flickered for a moment and then shone brightly, each separate bulb twinkling against the night sky.

A cheer went up from the crowd and then a crash of applause. For a minute, my throat tightened with emotion at the beauty and tradition before me. I was a total sucker for a moment like this, I admit it. This was one of the reasons I'd moved back home from Chicago. This feeling of warmth and belonging. Ravenmist might be a little crazy and possibly headed for an apocalypse but it was my town. I couldn't help but be filled with pride.

Sneaking a glance at Jack, I could swear his eyes were a little glassy but it just might have been the cold.

Yep, it was probably just the cold.

We were all sort of taking everything in, absorbing the Christmas spirit, when Iris Martin ran out of the civic center screaming. She hopped up onto the dais, her eyes like saucers and her chest heaving. She was pale and sort of looked like she'd been pulled through a hedge. Backward.

Frank grabbed her by the upper arms and gave her a little shake as no one could understand what she was saying. Finally, she slumped against the microphone, fat tears rolling down her cheeks.

"They're gone."

She hadn't spoken loudly, but she was right in front of the microphone so her words were boomed over the crowd as if she'd screamed them into a megaphone.

"They're gone," she repeated. "They were there before the play started, but now they're gone."

"What's gone?" Frank asked, accepting a water bottle from someone in the crowd and handing it to Iris. "What are you talking about?"

"The Farraday diaries. They're gone. Someone has stolen them."

So much for peace on earth and goodwill toward anyone.

Chapter Five

IRIS WAS CRYING. Her mother Natalie was trying to comfort her while Frank, Elliott, and Lloyd huddled together in the foyer of the civic center, pale and silent.

Jack was grim-faced and clearly not a happy camper. He'd called in every deputy he had to search each person at the tree-lighting ceremony to make sure they weren't trying to sneak out with the diaries. So far, they'd found nothing.

How could this have even happened? Why would this happen?

Wait...Arthur Cambridge and his daughter. They'd wanted to buy the diaries. Were they desperate enough to try and steal them? Where were they, anyway? I'd seen them earlier but I couldn't find them now.

I circled the area but couldn't find them anywhere. As far as I was concerned, they were suspect number one.

Except now I couldn't find Jack anymore, either. The crowd was beginning to thin now that the deputies had searched almost everyone. Where was he? This was a crime scene, for heaven's sake and he was a cop. Wasn't he supposed to be here sniffing out clues and calling for forensics?

From what I could see, he'd left Deputy Tim in charge, and nothing against Tim, but he'd once scored a touchdown for the opposing team because he'd been running the wrong way. Later he'd told people that he was dizzy. Tim was currently standing in front of the civic center's front doors and telling people that no one could go inside. He'd also stretched some yellow crime scene tape around the door handles.

"Where's Jack?"

Missy tugged at my jacket, appearing out of nowhere, and causing me to jump at the sound of her voice.

"Hey, you scared me. Where have you been? We were supposed to meet here."

"My grandmother called. She needed to see me right away." Missy's gaze ran over the now almost-empty town square. "I heard someone say that the diaries were stolen. Is that true?"

"It's true."

I didn't tell her that I suspected the Cambridges. It was only a gut feeling. I didn't have any proof.

"So…where is Jack?" Missy's gaze searched far over the plaza. "Shouldn't he be bossing around his deputies?"

"You'd think, but I actually don't know where he is. I was looking for him when you showed up." Her earlier words finally penetrated my brain. "Did you say your grandmother called? Is she okay?"

Missy's grandma was in excellent health – and supernatural – but she could probably still fall and break a hip or something.

"She's fine. She said she's had a premonition. Something big is about to happen in Ravenmist."

Groaning, I pressed fingers to my now throbbing temples. "That's fabulous news. *Not.* I don't suppose she knows what this big thing is going to be?"

"She doesn't. Just that she's felt a change in energy." Missy rubbed at the back of her neck. "Tedi, I feel it, too. It's almost like electrical charges all over my skin. It's weird but she's right. It's a sense of foreboding that I can't shake. I've felt it all evening."

My initial reaction was that we'd run out of time. It was the apocalypse and there was nothing we could do about it. My second reaction, though, was that the world hadn't ended yet so we still had…a chance. It was a slim one but hey, I was an optimist, right? Or at least trying to be.

"You haven't said anything," Missy prompted. "What are you thinking?"

"That we have a huge problem. What…if it's starting now?"

"I don't think so. I don't feel it. Not yet. Don't ask me how I know this, but I don't think this is the apocalypse. It's something, but it's not that."

"Your intuition talking? I'm not being sarcastic either because believe me, I want to believe that you're right."

"I guess it is intuition. But that's not all Grandma told me. I haven't told you the most exciting part."

"Dying in an apocalypse isn't the most exciting part? Do tell."

"One of her friends came through with a spell to help us identify the demon."

I swear I could hear angels singing. Did we just catch a break? And none too soon, either.

"Hallelujah, that's the best news I've had all day. Heck, maybe all week. When can we do it? Tonight?"

"Whoa, let's take one step at a time. We need to read through it and gather the items we need. This isn't like the spell your mom got off the internet to help Daisy's broken heart. This is a universe altering kind of thing. It's big and frankly, I'm not sure we're powerful enough to pull it off. Neither of us are witches."

"What about your grandmother? Can she help?"

"She can but remember, she's not a witch either. We're Reapers and that's totally different."

"We don't have a choice. We have to try."

Missy pulled a folded-up piece of paper from her coat pocket. "I have it here and I've read through it. It's very complex. I'll study it more closely and make a list of the supplies we'll need. Why don't we meet at Daisy's in the morning for breakfast? She'll be back from vacation by then. We could use her help on this. Maybe your mom, too."

We had to do whatever we could to save the world. No pressure.

I WAS EXHAUSTED by the time I returned to the inn, mind and body. My head was still swirling from all that had happened from the diaries being stolen, to Missy's grandmother's premonition, and to top it all off, a spell that would hopefully reveal the identity of the demon in Ravenmist. Had it only been yesterday that we'd been putting up the tree?

My feet were headed in the direction of the kitchen because I needed something sweet, like a piece of chocolate cake or maybe a slice of coconut cream pie – whatever we had in the refrigerator – but the sound of voices in the dining room had me changing direction. Reluctantly. One of those voices was Jack and the other two sounded suspiciously like Arthur and Belinda Cambridge.

Now I knew why Jack had left the crime scene. He was confronting the people who had the most motive to steal the diaries. I should have predicted this. I might have an issue with the mood that Jack had been lately but I couldn't fault his cop behavior.

The three of them stopped talking when I walked into the dining room. They were sitting at a round table near the windows and Jack and Arthur stood up when I approached. Because of the tree-lighting, I'd opted to close the restaurant for the evening and give everyone the night off.

"Jack, can I get any of you some coffee?"

"That would be great–"

"We're done here." Arthur's booming voice interrupted Jack's reply. "We're not going to be answering any more of your questions, Sheriff. If you want to speak to us, you can talk to my attorney first."

Belinda stood, as well, her color high. "That's right. Talk to our attorney. We don't have to take this sort of harassment."

With that pronouncement, the Cambridges marched out of the dining room, leaving Jack and I standing there.

"You sure know how to endear people to you, Jack. You're winning friends and influencing people all over town."

Groaning, he scraped his fingers through his short dark hair. "It's been a long day. I could use some coffee. And maybe some pie."

"Let's go into the kitchen and see what we have. I gave everyone the night off so we'll have to fend for ourselves."

All the lights were off in the kitchen, so I had to flip them on to see anything. Jack settled on a stool at the counter while I rummaged in the refrigerator, finally pulling out half a chocolate cake.

"Success! It's cake instead of pie, is that okay?

"No issues here. How about we get two forks and go at it?"

Knowing Jack's appetite he could put this cake away in one sitting.

"I thought you wanted coffee, too?"

"I can do without it. I'm fine with water."

Two forks and two glasses of water later, we were both sitting at the counter devouring the delicious devil's food cake as if we hadn't eaten in days. I couldn't speak for Jack, but I'd had a filling dinner only hours ago. Honestly, he was eating most of the cake. I still had no idea where he put all the food. He was trim and didn't have a spare ounce on him. As far as I knew, he didn't hit the gym, either. I'd never seen him so much as jog.

"Go ahead and ask, Tedi. I know the price of a meal in your kitchen by now."

Information was the price and Jack was always stingy with it. Unless he was shoving forkfuls of food in his mouth.

"Fine," I sniffed. "What did the Cambridges have to say?"

"Exactly what I expected them to say. That they didn't do it and that multiple people saw them sitting in the audience at the play. Then they threatened my job."

I could only imagine how that went over with Jack. He didn't take kindly to that sort of tactic.

"If it makes you feel any better, they did that to me as well."

"I have a feeling that we're part of an extremely non-exclusive group. They seemed quite comfortable threatening to sue me and ruin my life."

I glanced over my shoulder at the door to the dining room. "Do you think they're upstairs packing their stuff to make a run for it?"

Jack chuckled. "Make a run for it? Interesting turn of phrase. According to them, they're staying here through Monday morning."

"And you believe them?"

"At this point, I don't have any choice. I called my buddy in Chicago and he's checking them out for me, getting more background for when I talk to them again."

"Again?" I echoed. "They said they didn't want to talk to you."

"I think they're going to want to talk to me."

"You're certainly not lacking in self-confidence."

"Fear is the mind-killer. You have to believe in yourself."

"And now you're the Dalai Lama."

That made him laugh. "I'm as far from him as I can be."

Jack placed the fork on the edge of the empty plate. Somehow, he'd managed to scarf most of the cake down when I wasn't looking. Just as well, as it was the season of putting on an extra five pounds and I needed to pace myself. Thanksgiving was only two days ago. There were still several weeks – and many pies and casseroles – to go.

Standing, Jack pulled his car keys from his pocket. "I need to get going. Tyler's home alone and although I know he prefers it, I like to fool myself every now and then that he likes spending time with his old man."

"I'm sure that he does."

"Now you're just being polite. Did you like spending time with your parents when you were a teenager?"

"I did," I protested. "It was my sisters that I wanted to avoid."

"How is it that I've never met your sisters?"

"You've been lucky?"

"If they're anything like you, your parents had their hands full."

Tilting my head, I gave him a narrow-eyed look. "You know

I never know how to take it when you say things like that. Is that an insult? Is it a compliment? I can't really tell."

He moved toward the door. "It's a compliment. When I insult someone, there's no doubt."

Yep, that sounded like Jack.

I shut the kitchen lights out and followed Jack to the front door, through the empty dining room and quiet lobby. My night manager Anna sat at the desk studying, but pretty much everyone else had retired to their rooms.

Pushing the door open, Jack stepped outside and for some reason I followed him even though I wasn't wearing a coat. The chill of November immediately penetrated my sweater and I wrapped my arms around my torso for warmth.

Instead of walking back inside. After the day I'd had, my mind was officially mush.

"Goodnight, Jack. I better go in–"

"Look," he interrupted my graceful departure, pointing up to the sky. "Look up there."

It was a starry night and at first, I thought he was pointing out the Big Dipper because it was clearly visible, but then I saw what he was really referring to.

A shooting star. In the night sky. Just like in the movies, and just as breathtaking and beautiful.

"Make a wish," he said in my ear, resting a hand on each of my shoulders. "Make it a good one because that's one heck of a star."

I need to find out the identity of the demon so we can stop the apocalypse.

The star was bright with a long tail, but it was gone as quickly as it had come, disappearing into the horizon, leaving me standing there in the freezing cold and wondering if I'd even really seen it.

I'd only mailed my letter to Santa that morning. There was no way he would have received it yet but...

It had to be a coincidence. A strange and wonderful coincidence. Life was full of them, after all. Right?

"Did you make a wish?"

I nodded, still bemused by the entire situation. A shooting star. Hmmm...perhaps I needed to hang out in the cold more often.

"Did you, Jack?"

"I certainly did."

"What did you wish for?"

I don't know why I asked the question because he was far too stubborn to ever answer.

"The usual. Peace on earth."

"That's a good wish."

Jack didn't have a clue just how good it was. We'd basically wished for the same thing, albeit by different routes.

I could only hope that somehow we'd managed to convince the universe to grant us a wish. Just one.

Chapter Six

I WAS PUTTING on lipstick the next morning in my bathroom when I heard Terrence in the living room working on the laptop I'd given him. With all the supernatural energy in Ravenmist, he'd been out and about more often and was now rarely at home. It was certainly a change from the shy and more introverted spirit I'd first met last year. Frankly, his social life was better than mine. I'd heard a rumor he was…dating.

Thankfully the female in question was also a ghost. Since Amelia and Charles were married last spring, ghosts had been dating and falling in love in rather shocking numbers. It was kind of sweet, though, that they didn't let the afterlife deter them from finding true love.

"I'm going out to breakfast with Missy," I said, shrugging on my coat. It was another chilly day outside. "I'll be back later, though. What are your plans for the day?"

"I guess I'll do a few minor edits to the documentary…since I don't have a job or any actual responsibilities."

Sigh. I was going to have to find something for him to do. Soon.

"The bookstore is closed today so I know that Edward has the day off. Maybe you two can do something together."

"He's doing inventory for Missy today."

That sly minx. She'd outsourced her quarterly inventory to a ghost. I had to admire her ingenuity. Wait...I had inventory, too.

"I have a few ideas about jobs you can do around here. I just need time to figure it all out."

Terrence visibly brightened. "Really? I really want to help."

"I know you do and I think you'll be a great addition to the team. Just give me a day or two more to get the details in line."

"I will. Thanks, Tedi."

I reached for my purse but my hand hesitated. There was a question I wanted to ask.

"Terrence, were you at the play and tree-lighting last night?"

"I've been there every year since I was a kid. This year's play was better than usual."

I agreed.

"Did you happen to see anyone around the artifacts room? Like the Cambridges?"

Terrence shook his head. "When I saw them they were sitting watching the play. I did see Natalie Martin hovering around the door most of the time. Does that help? Do you think she stole the diaries?"

Natalie? No. Although she had been rather adamant that the Farraday clan wasn't capable of taking care of them. Was she so convinced that she'd gone to the drastic step of *stealing* them? I couldn't imagine it. That was a bridge too far even for Natalie Martin.

"I don't think her motive is as strong as the Cambridges."

"Are they still in the hotel?"

"Until tomorrow morning. Unless Jack can convince them to stay longer."

If he didn't have any evidence, though, he wouldn't be able to. We'd been down this road before.

Bidding my ghostly roommate goodbye, I headed to Daisy's to meet Missy. When I got there, Missy and Daisy were already sitting in a booth near the front window, their heads close together. I assumed that Missy was bringing our friend up to date on the latest news.

About the world ending and all.

We hugged and I slid into the booth next to Missy. A cup of hot coffee was placed in front of me almost magically. Everyone here knew of my major caffeine addiction. Personally, I preferred to call it caffeine *enthusiasm*.

"I told Daisy everything," Missy stated after the waitress took our order and disappeared into the kitchen. "She agrees that we need to loop in your mother. We're going to need her help with the spell at the very least."

Just because my mother had pulled a spell off the internet and helped cast it so that Daisy's heart wasn't broken anymore didn't mean she knew anything about real witchcraft. She was Presbyterian, for heaven's sake. A lapsed one, but still...

"I'm not sure that my mother is ready to hear that the world might end because of a fight between good and evil."

Daisy's brows shot up. "You want her to be unprepared? That seems harsh. You were planning on telling her last spring but that was interrupted when she found the gun in the movie theater. What's changed your mind?"

"I was sort of going with the idea that ignorance was bliss," I explained. "I know that the world might end and some days I wished I didn't. Everyone else, on the other hand, is just living their best lives completely unaware that they could be eating that last cookie and not worrying about their diet."

Missy nodded soberly. "You do have a point there."

"I know."

Daisy still didn't look convinced. "According to Missy, the spell is very complex. We really need the help. Plus, none of us are real witches so we need all the thoughts and power we can get to make it work."

Real witches. Like real unicorns? Were witches actually real? At this point, anything was possible. I had to suppose that if Missy's grandmother had a spell that the existence of actual witches was probably a given.

"Fine, I will tell my mother that the world might end soon. I don't suppose either of you have any ideas how to cushion that blow?"

"I've been thinking about that since Missy told me this morning," Daisy said. "I think that I should tell Peggy. I'm her peer and I think it will come better from me than from her daughter."

I was totally and completely onboard with letting some other victim – oops! I mean person – take on this job, but it felt like I was chickening out. I didn't like to think of myself as lily-livered.

"I appreciate the offer but I think this is something that I should probably be doing. I don't want to push this off on anyone else."

"You're not pushing. I'm offering. I really do think it would be best, Tedi. Can you trust me to do this?"

I'd trust Daisy to do just about anything so I gracefully acquiesced. I didn't know what she had planned but it had to be better than what I had.

Nothing. Nada. Zip-o-roni.

Our food came out and we didn't speak until we were alone again. We might be ready to reveal our secrets to my mother but not to the general population.

Can you say *panic in the streets*?

"Did Jack talk to the Cambridges?" Daisy asked, digging into her bacon and eggs. I'd ordered the waffles and Missy the ham and cheese omelet. "Those two are a real piece of work if you ask me."

"When did you meet them?"

She made a face like her breakfast wasn't good. "They were here early this morning. Nasty and demanding. Treated everyone like they were servants. I know that type. I suggested that they eat somewhere else while they were in town."

"How'd they take that?"

"I didn't stick around to find out. I held the door open and they went through it, moaning and complaining the entire time. It must be exhausting to be that unhappy about life."

"They have the strongest motive," Missy said in between bites of her omelet. "They wanted the diaries and were angry about them not being for sale."

I agreed…but I'd been thinking about that…

"They had to know that they'd be the main suspects when the diaries disappeared. Especially after throwing a tantrum with the Farraday family. If I were planning to steal something, I wouldn't make a scene in front of the sheriff a few hours before."

"Maybe it was an impulse," Missy suggested. "They didn't plan it but saw the opportunity and took it."

"Do you think they're innocent?" Daisy asked. "You look conflicted."

I felt conflicted. I didn't like the Cambridges. At all. But that didn't make them criminals.

"I agree that they have the strongest motive, but I talked to Terrence this morning. He said that he saw Natalie Martin hanging around the door to the archive room during the play."

Missy's brows pinched together. "You're thinking that Natalie Martin stole the diaries? Why on earth would she do that?"

"I'm not saying that she did. I'm saying that Terrence saw her there by the door. Think about it. If she was standing there, how could the Cambridges get in? She would have said something to Jack if they'd tried to get by her." I paused, hating myself for saying the next words. "She does have motive, though. She thinks that the Farradays aren't taking care of the diaries."

"So you do think she might have done it?" Daisy asked, glancing around the diner to make sure no one was listening in. "It is possible. I like Natalie but she's an odd duck. You just never know about people. But honestly? My money is on the Cambridges. That room in the civic center has a back door. They could have snuck in that way when no one was paying any attention, probably when everyone was moving from the auditorium outside to the tree."

That back door. I'd forgotten about it. Anyone could have come in and stolen the diaries.

I threw up my hands in frustration. "We may never know who did it."

Missy gave me a reproving look. "Have some faith in Jack. I would think you'd have more confidence in him. You're his best friend, after all."

I was Jack's best friend? When had that happened?

Daisy nodded in agreement. "You could do worse, you know."

"That's what everyone says. I hope you think the same for him." I took a deep breath. "Now how about this spell? What do we need to do?"

Missy pulled a piece of paper out of her jacket pocket and placed it in the center of the table.

"It's really two spells," she explained. "The first part is what's called a scry spell and the second is called Isolde's answer. Basically, the first spell gives the identity of the demon and the second makes the answer of the first clearer so it can be read."

"Scry?" Daisy repeated. "Is that a real word?"

"It is," Missy confirmed. "It's a sort of divination spell. In this case the spell uses a mirror to answer our question. Then the second spell temporarily enhances the magical mirror. We can ask the mirror a single question and the answer will show in the mirror."

"That doesn't sound too difficult," I said. Frankly, I was relieved that it was so straightforward. I had fears of sacrificing chickens or goats. "We say some magic words and presto-chango we've got an answer."

Missy shook her head. "It's not that easy. First, we have to gather all of the supplies and find just the right place to cast the spell. If we don't find the exact right spot, it won't work. One mistake and we get nothing. Second, and this is something we all need to think about, is that once the spell is cast, the demon will know right away about the spell."

Okay, maybe it wasn't going to be so easy. This sounded...tricky. And perhaps a little dangerous.

"If the demon isn't from the good side, this could be a major problem," Daisy said nervously. "I'm not sure that I like the sound of this."

"We're making a huge assumption that the demon is good," Missy agreed. "Because of the amount of energy they've brought to Ravenmist and also that nothing really bad has happened yet. We could be wrong."

Did evil demons have bad tempers? Just how upset would they be?

Missy went on. "My grandmother also pointed out that we're assuming that there's one demon and only one. If there's more, the mirror will only show an image of one of them."

"Which one will they show?" I asked, my breakfast completely abandoned at this point. My stomach was churning with nerves.

"It depends on how we ask our one question, but grandma said that the mirror may just show us the demon in the closest physical proximity."

The thought of an evil demon being anywhere close to me had me shuddering in my seat.

"But we've always assumed that it was one demon," I pointed out. "We have no evidence that there's more than that."

"True," Missy conceded. "I just wanted to point out that the spell is very specific. It's going to be based on how we ask our single question. We can't just ask it to show the demon. That's too generic."

"Then we need to ask it to show us the demon that's brought all the energy to Ravenmist," I replied. "Or should we ask it to show us all demons in Ravenmist?"

Missy held up her index finger. "We get one question. We just need to make sure it's a good one."

"The universe is very picky," I sniffed. "You would think it might cut us some slack. We're trying to help."

"The universe is neutral," Missy said with a shrug. "It doesn't care more about good or evil. It's Switzerland in all of this."

"So where does that leave us?" Daisy asked. "What do we need to do next?"

Missy tapped the paper. "We need to start gathering the supplies for the spells, and then find a place that's quiet, private, and out of the way to cast it. The spell has specific instructions on the kind of place we need."

I pulled out my phone ready to make a list. "Okay, I'm ready. Go for it."

"A large bonfire, a pool of still water, a mass of clouds, a section of smooth stones, and a quiet grove of trees. We'll also need a bowl of red ink and a smooth mirror floating in it."

"That's...weird."

Daisy nodded. "I agree. We can easily build a bonfire on a cloudy night in a quiet grove of trees but finding a pool of still water and a section of smooth stones isn't going to be a piece of cake."

"That's just for the first spell," Missy replied with a sigh. "The second is...more complicated."

From the expression my friend wore this wasn't good.

"Such as?"

"The bark of a paperbark maple tree."

That didn't sound like the end of the world. I'd never heard of it but if it existed then we could get it, right?

"And then?"

Missy rubbed at her temple. "Flesh of a mammal."

Say...what?

"Flesh of a mammal? Do you mean like...meat?"

"I guess so." Missy pointed to the paper. "That's what it says. It doesn't say what kind. I don't know if they mean chicken, cow, goat, or something else. This is what I was talking about. One misstep and we're toast."

Daisy held up her hands in a surrender motion. "Fine, fine. We need the flesh of a mammal. What else?"

"A waning moon, dried chamomile blossoms, powdered ginger, peppermint oil, and the petal of a newly opened rose."

"Just another Saturday night at the grocery store," I said, sarcasm dripping from my tone. Why couldn't anything be easy? "What...no batwing or wolfsbane?"

"Wolfsbane is poisonous," Daisy said. "We should just be glad that all of these supplies are actually something that we can obtain. I was afraid it was going to ask for the feather from a golden goose that speaks Spanish."

Neither Missy or I had a chance to reply. My phone began to vibrate and I quickly checked my texts, surprised to find one from Jack.

"I didn't expect to hear from him this morning...Jack just sent me a text."

Missy leaned over to try and read over my shoulder. "What does it say? Did he ask you out on a date again?"

Missy was the only one that knew about Jack's first invitation.

Daisy immediately perked up and I wanted to crawl under the table. "Again? Has Jack asked you out before? How did I not know this?"

I elbowed Missy in the ribs. Hard. "You didn't know because it didn't happen. Missy is just joking. And no, Jack is not asking me on a date. He's asking if he can use my drawing room to question a few people. According to this text, he wants to keep it informal and he doesn't want to bring them down to the station."

"Are you going to say yes?" Daisy asked.

Definitely.

"I'm already typing out my reply."

Jack's reply came back lightning fast.

Thanks. I assumed you'd say yes, so I already told them to meet me there in about an hour.

That was our Jack. Give him an inch and he thought he was a ruler.

"We need to talk about this spell and do it quickly. We don't know how much time we have left."

Missy pointed to herself and then Daisy. "We're on it. We'll work on it this morning. Why don't we meet up later and we can go through it?"

They had a plan. Now I needed to shove the rest of this breakfast down my throat and get home. I wanted to hear what these suspects – whoever they were – had to say for themselves.

I really did believe in Jack. He'd find out who did this.

Chapter Seven

I'D BARELY WALKED in the front door of the inn when Tina at the front desk waved me down. She had that look on her face that she always gets when Jack was here. So clearly, he'd arrived before me.

"The sheriff is here," she said without preamble. "He's in the drawing room. Apparently, Natalie and Iris Martin will be here in about ten minutes."

"It's okay," I assured her. "He asked me. I should have called to let you know."

"It's fine. He was very polite when he talked to me."

That was good to hear. Maybe he was in a decent mood today.

Hey, it could happen.

"You have a package."

I'd sort of tuned Tina out but her statement pulled me out of my thoughts.

"A package? It's Sunday."

Tina shrugged and held out a rectangular box. The kind for shirts or pants. "A delivery van pulled up and I had to sign for it.

It has your name on it so it's definitely for you."

I accepted it and went into my apartment to open it. As far as I could remember, I hadn't ordered anything, although wine and too much late-night television could be a killer combination with a valid credit card.

The sender was Simpson's department store. I was positive that I hadn't ordered anything from them. Using a letter opener, I cut open the shiny packing tape and opened the box which, of course, had another smaller box inside of it. This time the name of the department store was splashed on the top in bold script. I opened the box and then pulled back the tissue paper to reveal...

The seafoam green sweater that I had been admiring in the window.

That I'd put on my Christmas list. This was two items now that had tick marks next to them. What on earth? I'd just mailed that letter and there was no way Santa could have even received it by now. But...

Here it was. The sweater that I'd coveted. Right here in front of me. It was real because I could feel the incredibly soft cashmere under my fingertips. It was positively decadent and I couldn't wait to wear it. Except that I didn't know who to thank. My mother had always been a stickler for thank you notes and we weren't allowed to wear or use a gift until they were sent.

There had to be a card here somewhere, but I practically shredded both boxes and the tissue paper and there was none. How strange. If I were going to send someone a gift, I'd surely want them to know it was from me. Maybe Simpson's forgot?

That was it. They must have forgotten to put the card in the box. I'd call them in the morning and simply ask who sent it. Easy peasy. Then I'd write the thank you note and wear my gorgeous new sweater.

While shopping for a gift for whomever sent this one.

I tucked the sweater back into the box and placed it on my bed. I'd try it on later. Right now, I needed to find out what was going on with Jack's investigation.

Now the Ravenmist Inn is over one hundred years old and has had many renovations over the years. One of them was a major addition to the main building and that's how my apartment on the ground floor came into existence. Consequently, there was a window in my walk-in closet that had once been on the exterior of the house and it led directly to the drawing room. My grandmother had placed a drape on the drawing room side and no one was the wiser that my closet was on the other side. I could hear everything going on in there and Jack had no idea.

Climbing over my winter boots, I sat down on an old suitcase that I used to store my summer clothes, and leaned against the wall right under the window. Just in the nick of time. I could hear Jack greeting Natalie and Iris.

"I suppose you want to talk about last night. I'm not sure that we can tell you anymore than we already have."

That was Natalie's voice. She didn't sound happy about being summoned.

"I'd like to review what happened last night, if you don't

mind," Jack replied, his tone neutral. He was better at that than just about anyone I knew. He could make a fortune playing poker if he had the inclination. "You might remember something today that you didn't last night."

"I have an excellent memory," Natalie sniffed. "I told you everything last night."

"You said that you watched the play, is that correct?"

"It is. I watch the play every year."

"A few people reported to me last night that they saw you standing by the door to the artifacts room during the play."

Silence. Natalie Martin wasn't the type to not say anything. Finally, she responded.

"I was there…for a short while."

"Were you meeting someone?"

"No, that wasn't it."

I heard the sound of footsteps grow closer to the wall and then Iris spoke up.

"Mother, just tell the sheriff the truth. Sheriff, my mother was worried about the safety of the artifacts. I told her she didn't need to be but it turns out she was right after all."

The last was said in a bitter tone. Poor Iris. Her whole life was wrapped up in the history of the town and now this had happened on her watch.

"Of course, I was right. Those Farradays can't be trusted to take care of important historical documents such as the diaries. They should donate them to the town."

"Mother!"

Jack loudly cleared his throat. "Excuse me, can we get back to the facts? How you feel about the Farradays, Mrs. Martin, is your business. But unless you believe they stole their own property I don't think it should be part of this conversation."

"It was that Arthur Cambridge," Natalie said hotly. "He's the one, you can bet on it. He wanted those diaries and I bet he stole them. I saw him watching me when I was standing by the door. That's why I never sat down to watch the play. I just knew he was waiting for me to walk away and then he was going to steal something."

"So you didn't walk away?"

"Exactly."

"So he didn't steal anything."

"Well..."

"Someone could have gone in the back door, Sheriff," Iris said. "It was locked but I suppose that wouldn't stop a criminal."

"It wouldn't," Jack agreed. "A locked door probably would have only slowed him or her down slightly. Now is there anything else that you remember from last night? Was Arthur Cambridge the only one hanging around or was there anyone else? Also, aside from you, Iris, who else has keys to that room?"

Another long silence.

"Elliott," Iris finally said with a sigh. She sounded rather reluctant to have revealed that detail. "Elliott Farraday. He has keys to the entire civic center because of the play."

There was an audible snort that I was pretty sure came from Natalie. She sure had a bee in her bonnet about the Farrday family.

I'D SNUCK OUT of the closet and into the kitchen for a cup of coffee and that's where Jack found me. I was slugging down a coffee and a cinnamon roll and by the look on his face, he was going to want one, too. I didn't even bother to ask him. I just slapped one on a plate and handed him a fork.

"How did it go?" I asked, oh so casually. He had no idea that I'd listened in. "Did you learn anything from Iris and Natalie?"

He shoved a huge bite into his mouth so it took him awhile to answer. "I did, but somehow I think you already know about it."

"Me?"

I looked suitably innocent, as if butter wouldn't melt in my mouth.

"You," he confirmed with a chuckle. "I wouldn't put it past you to have wired the drawing room for sound. Not that I would care if you did. If you want to know something, Tedi, you know by now that all you have to do is ask. I've learned that the gossip mill is wicked in town and at least I'm telling you what really happened. It wouldn't hurt to have the truth be spread about."

I could feel the color rise in my cheeks. "I'm shocked that you think I would do something as underhanded and sneaky as wire the drawing room. It's a mean thing to say, Jack Garrett. I don't gossip either."

He grinned as if my scolding meant nothing to him. "I know I'm in trouble when you use my whole name. Now do you want to hear about it or not?"

"I do," I sighed loudly. "But you could be nicer about it."

He took the last bite of cinnamon roll. "Let me see…how to keep this short and to the point. Natalie admitted that she stood by the door all evening. She thinks Arthur Cambridge and his daughter probably stole the diaries. Iris blames herself. And they think the thief had to come through the back door to the room. Right…and also that Elliott Farraday has a key to all of the doors in the civic center."

Elliott did have keys but Natalie had left a fact or two out of her statement.

"He does have keys, but so do a lot of people, Jack."

"Such as?"

"Every member of the town council plus the janitorial crew. Maybe more, for all I know. I guess what I'm saying is that getting a copy of that key would be easy. It's not an exclusive club."

Jack frowned. "Wait…that means that Natalie Martin has a set of keys. At least, her husband does."

"She definitely has access. Let's face it, Jack, it's not like this town has mad skills when it comes to security issues. Most of us don't even lock our doors."

He growled, clearly from frustration. "That makes me crazy. Lock your doors. It's common sense. This isn't Mayberry and I'm not Andy Griffith. There are people in this world that are evil, Tedi. I wish you would believe me when I say that."

"I do believe you."

Because I knew that he was right. Evil was out there and ready to fight with the forces of good. Would we win?

His expression softened. "I'm glad you believe me. I know that you all want to believe that nothing bad is ever going to happen here, but it would be naive to think that."

"So are you going to talk to Elliott? He was there but he was busy with the play all night. He was backstage."

Jack rubbed at the back of his neck where I'm sure he had a permanent pain from dealing with our town. "Honestly, I don't think so. I agree that he was backstage because Tyler mentioned that Elliott stayed in the wings the entire performance to make sure no one missed their cue or if anyone forgot their lines. I guess he could have given his keys to someone else, but it sounds like everyone in this town could have gotten their hands on them. I'm going to have to hope that the security cameras around the building picked something or someone up on tape."

Wait…there was video?

"Security cameras? When did they put those in? I don't remember seeing them."

A slow smile crossed Jack's face. "I know. I convinced the town council about six months ago that having more security for the historical artifacts would be a good idea."

I rolled my eyes. "Okay, you're brilliant. And a little clairvoyant, which is creepy. But if you have this video, then why are you even talking to Natalie and Iris? Just look at the video and see if someone came in the back entrance."

"I've already looked at it. It's terrible footage. It's far too dark to see much but two figures walking around. I sent it to my buddy in Chicago and he's going to have a friend of his try to enhance the video, but that friend is out of town for the holiday weekend."

"Two people? But you can't see who it is?"

Jack drained the last of his coffee and stood. "I cannot, so I have to wait and hope. In the meantime, I'm trying to narrow down who it might be. I may have to give up and just wait."

"Then the Cambridges might get away. I mean…if they did it, that is."

"So you've decided that they're guilty?"

I hadn't. But they had motive.

"No."

"But you're worried they're going to get away?"

"If they did do it, which I'm not saying that they did. But by the time you see the video they could be long gone. You did say that you saw two figures. That could be Arthur and his daughter."

"Or two completely different individuals."

"That, too."

"As for them being long gone, that's a chance we take with everyone that comes into town. I'm hoping to see the video before they leave but if not, I can't help that. At that point they'll be fugitives."

"You don't think they did it."

He sighed and shook his head. "I don't know, Tedi. Frankly, I don't have a clue who did it and that doesn't make me happy, by the way. Arthur Cambridge and his daughter certainly have motive but it's iffy on opportunity."

"Elliott Farraday may have a key to the civic center but it doesn't make any sense to steal his own family's diaries."

"That's true. That's why I'm not running off to talk to him. He has zero motive and not much opportunity."

"So who does that leave?"

"Unfortunately, it leaves Natalie and Iris Martin. Clearly, the mother has huge issues with the Farradays."

"Iris doesn't."

"But she had opportunity. A great deal of it. Right now, I'm looking at them along with the Cambridges."

"Iris didn't do this, Jack."

It felt like he and I had this discussion far too often.

"That's good news. Then she'll have no problem when I search her home and vehicle."

Oh my stars.

"Jack, did you get search warrants?"

I couldn't even say the words out loud. I'd whispered them.

"I did and I'm not sorry, Tedi. I'm searching the Cambridges, too. I'm just waiting on the judge to sign the paperwork. He's been out of town for the holiday."

This just might get ugly.

Chapter Eight

G ROUND GINGER IS easy to find, as is peppermint oil. The petal of a rose? Piece of cake. Dried chamomile flowers? A little more difficult.

The bark of a paperbark maple? A real challenge.

That's why Missy and Daisy set out early the next morning to travel thirty minutes to the nearest city that had a large nursery with unusual trees. We could have ordered it over the internet but it would have taken at least a week, maybe more. We were hoping to do the spell tonight.

The sooner, the better as far as we were concerned.

So my mother Peggy Hamilton and I were scouting for the perfect location to do the spell. We needed a quiet grove of trees, a still pool of water, and smooth, natural stones, along with the mass of clouds.

The weather was supposed to cooperate this evening, and it was a waning moon. If we didn't do it in the next few days, we'd have to wait for another moon cycle.

My mother had dragged me out into the cold at dawn – let me repeat that – *at dawn* to check out an area that she and Dad used to go to when they were dating. We couldn't park the car close so we had to walk. Of course. The weather was cold and overcast, the wind sharp. I was wrapped up in a coat, scarf, and gloves and I was still cold.

"I'm cold, Mom."

"I know, dear. You're always cold. Are you wearing a sweater under your coat?"

"I am." This might be a good time to ask her about the sweater I received. Maybe she sent it. "I got a present in the mail yesterday. It was a green cashmere sweater from Simpson's. I don't suppose you sent it? It didn't have a card."

Shivering, I stuck my hands into my pockets as we tromped through the woods. I was operating on one cup of coffee this morning, hastily gulped down before we left the inn. I would have given my brown leather boots that cost me the earth for a cup of coffee right this minute.

And a Danish.

Maybe some bacon.

"A sweater? No, I haven't actually been Christmas shopping yet. I have an outing planned this week. You should go with me. I'm heading up to Chicago."

I wasn't a big city girl anymore but I did love to shop in Chicago.

"Can we get deep dish pizza?"

"We can."

"Then I'm in. But if you didn't buy it, maybe Dad did. Or Missy. She saw me looking at it in the window display. It's probably Missy, now that I think about it. The card was probably just forgotten."

"I'm sure it was Missy. She always gets you the nicest presents. I hope you're going to get her something nice this year, Tedi. Cashmere is expensive."

No kidding. This sweater wasn't on sale, either. Which made me pause for a moment as I wondered why Missy would spend so much money on me. We didn't usually go crazy like that on holidays.

"I don't think that I've been getting Missy lousy gifts, Mom. I think I'm an excellent gift-giver."

I took great pride in trying to find the perfect gift for the recipient.

"Of course, you are," she replied in a soothing tone. "I always love your gifts to me."

"You're my mother. You have to say that."

"I don't. I'm at the age where I can just tell the truth. When you were little, I was obligated to lie but even then you chose lovely gifts. Your father was always good at gift-giving, too. I think you got that trait from him."

"Is he still dating–"

"I have no idea, Tedi, and it's not any of my business. We're getting a divorce."

About that…

"You've been getting a divorce for over a year now."

"These things take time."

"Mine didn't take long. We sold the condo and went our

separate ways."

Cue the marching band playing happy music.

"Your father and I have been married for many years, Tedi. We have more joint property and accounts than a simple condo."

"So...you're fighting over money?"

That didn't seem like my parents. They'd never even argued about money that I could remember. Mostly it was about my mom's mother, who was a real piece of work.

Peggy stopped and gave me that look. The one I remembered from when I was a teenager and I was asking her if I could go somewhere and she'd already told me no like a hundred times but I wasn't going to give up.

Yeah, that one. Except that I wasn't sixteen anymore and it didn't really work now.

"I think it's a fair question. You and Dad made a big announcement that you're getting a divorce and here it is more than a year later and it isn't done. You're both dating other people–"

"I'm not dating anyone."

"Well, he is. At least, I think he is. He went to Miami again over the summer."

Peggy sighed and rolled her eyes. "Your father isn't dating her anymore."

"How do you know?"

She crossed her arms over her chest, her lips pressed into a thin line. She was annoyed with me but she couldn't ground me anymore or make me clean the garbage cans. I was a grown woman and she'd told me to get okay with my parents getting a divorce. I'd done as they'd asked but so far, they weren't holding up their end of the bargain. Were they planning to drag this out and emotionally scar their daughter for life?

"Because he told me."

"Dad told you? That's...weird."

"We're friends. We were together a long time and that doesn't just disappear. Would you prefer it if we hated one another?"

"No, it just seems strange to me. I don't ever want to see David again."

David was my ex-husband.

"I swear, Theodosia Hamilton, you could find the muddy lining in a silver cloud. What happened to all that optimism you were going on and on about?"

A demon apocalypse. Evil versus good. Total destruction of humankind.

"I'm a work in progress, Mom."

"Your sisters are far more optimistic."

Good for them. They were constantly complaining that they were disappointed. I, on the other hand, was rarely disappointed.

"I think we need to change the subject. Are we close to this special spot?"

"Just a little farther," Mom replied, leading the way. "Through this cluster of trees, if I remember correctly. It's been a long time. Yes, this is it."

This was a small clearing surrounded by huge oak and maple trees in a U-shape. There was a small pond on my left and all the way to the back was a short wall of smooth stones that looked like at one time it might have been part of a fireplace.

"I think it was a cabin," Peggy said. "A long time ago, of course. When I was a teenager, we used to come out here and have bonfires and hang out. I think this fits all of our needs as long as it's cloudy tonight."

"I was a teenager once. How did I not know about this place?"

"You don't like to be cold."

Right. There was that.

"I wonder if Missy knows about it. She never gets cold."

"I described it to her and she wasn't familiar. Maybe your generation didn't hang out in the woods."

"It's perfect."

It was as if this spot was made specially for doing this spell. It met every criteria. Missy was going to be ecstatic.

"For once you're optimistic. I guess you like it."

"I do. We might just be able to pull this off."

Peggy and I hadn't talked about any of this situation.

"You know that this isn't yours to fix. You've taken all of this onto your own shoulders but you're only one person. If this is truly a fight between good and evil, well…that's way above your paygrade. Anyone's paygrade. We have to trust that good will win."

"I don't know if I can do that. I'm the pessimist in the family, remember?"

I tried to say it playfully but it didn't come out that way. It came out more...painful. Because this wasn't a laughing matter. It felt like there was a ticking time bomb somewhere but we simply couldn't find it.

"I know that you're doing everything that you can," Peggy replied quietly. "No one could ask you or Missy to do more. If the worst happens, then we'll be together. As a family."

It was a comforting thought but I wasn't even close to being ready to give up.

Evil better pack its bags. Ravenmist was going to fight back.

MY MOTHER AND I sent Daisy and Missy messages about how perfect the location was and to ask if they'd found the rest of the supplies. Luckily, they had so we met back at the diner mid-morning for a late breakfast and early lunch. I was starving from the brisk weather and dying for caffeine. We had a quick meetup to discuss logistics for that night and then – armed with a large coffee to go – I headed back to the inn. I had some work to do, plus I still needed to call Simpson's about the sender of that beautiful sweater.

I was halfway there when I noticed a handsome man standing on the sidewalk, seemingly lost. He was looking to the north, frowning, and then looking to the south. We get quite a few people like this in Ravenmist and they're always tourists trying to find their way.

"Can I help you? You look a little lost."

The man turned toward me and almost took my breath away. He was the epitome of tall, dark, and gorgeous. I mean…wow. Like male model-slash-actor level good-looking. I wasn't a pushover for guys like that. C'mon folks, I was past that stage, but I couldn't help being shocked to look someone that handsome right in the eye. Frankly, he was easy to look at.

He smiled and a dimple pierced his stubbled cheek. "I am a little lost. I was hoping you could point me toward The Grateful Raven. I'm told it has some of the best food in town."

"You've been told correctly. You're actually quite close. Just a block down on the left. Try the turkey dinner. It's fantastic."

He gave me another Hollywood-worthy smile. "I will, thank you. Nice town you have here. Really charming."

"Thank you. We like it."

"I can see why. I might stick around longer than I planned. Thank you again."

By the time I said you're welcome he was already heading down the sidewalk.

At the end of the block, I couldn't help but turn around to see if he had followed my simple instructions but he was nowhere to be seen. He must have moved incredibly fast to already be inside the diner. Perhaps he was cold and he'd jogged the rest of the way.

By the time I arrived on the front porch of the inn I was ready for a fresh coffee and a crackling fireplace to warm up my bones. I wanted to shed my heavy coat and scarf in my apartment but I stopped at the front desk to pick up my messages.

Another box had been delivered.

It had my name on it and it was from Simpson's. Because I'd been up so early with my mom, I hadn't even had a chance to call the retailer yet. Now I'd be calling about two deliveries.

Once again, I took it into my apartment and placed it on the kitchen table. The gift was in a smaller box, the item wrapped protectively in bubbled plastic.

It was the daringly red lipstick I'd coveted so much I'd put it on my Christmas list to Santa. It was amazingly crimson, almost dripping blood and I loved it. As a redhead I had to be careful with lipstick, but this shade was deep enough that it wouldn't make me look half-dead or that I had pneumonia. It was like finding a unicorn in a herd of donkeys.

But still. How on earth? This was getting weird. Just…weird. There was no other word for it. Even Missy didn't know about the lipstick. I'd been alone that day that I'd seen it. Any minute now I was going to hear "The Twilight Zone" theme music.

"Tedi?"

I looked up to find Terrence staring at me as if I had two heads, which at this point in my life wouldn't have surprised me in the least. Ravenmist was seriously getting strange.

I slid the gold tube back into the small box. "Sorry, I was a little distracted. Did you say something?"

"I said hello. About four times."

"I have a lot on my mind." Which wasn't a lie. "How are

you today?"

"I'm fine." His gaze ran over the open box and the packing materials. "Did you get something?"

"Yes, although I don't know who it's from. Just the same as the seafoam green sweater." A thought occurred to me. "I don't suppose it's from you?"

Terrence could make himself invisible, so it was completely possible that he'd watched me write the letter to Santa. Not probable because he'd never spied on me before.

But possible.

He shook his head, however. "Sorry. It's not. You don't know who it's from? What does the card say?"

"That's just it. There's no card. In either box. When I got the first one, I assumed it was an oversight but now I think it's on purpose. I'm going to have to call the department store and ask them who sent me this so I can send them a thank you card."

"They may not tell you."

"Why not? It's my gift."

Terrence pointed to the box. "It specifically didn't have a card. Perhaps the sender wants to remain anonymous. You might have a secret admirer."

The whole secret admirer thing was just the silliest. It was like the *blessing in disguise* stuff. If I were a blessing, I sure wouldn't wear a disguise. And having a secret admirer wasn't much better. Okay, maybe someone admires me from afar – I can always use the ego boost – but I can't do anything about it because they've kept their identity a secret. While it might also be sort of romantic, it had icky stalker vibes as well. All in all, I don't think being a secret admirer is a wise choice.

"I really hope not." I set the small box down on the table and faced my ghost in residence. "I've thought about the whole job thing and I've come up with one that I think you'd be good at. You're very detail-oriented and we need someone to do the weekly inventory. You'd count the towels, washcloths, sheets, soaps, shampoos. All that kind of stuff. Then you'd give it to me so I can order anything that we need. It would probably take you one day a week. That would give you plenty of time to work on your documentary. What do you say?"

Terrence's eyes lit up and he did a fist pump in the air. "That sounds great. When do I start?"

"We do inventory every Thursday so I can put in the order on Friday morning. This week we'll do it together and then you can let me know if you feel comfortable enough to do it on your own next week."

Squaring his shoulders, he nodded. "I won't let you down."

"I know you won't. You're going to do great."

"I'm going to the bookstore to tell Edward. Do you want to come?"

I did, but I needed to actually do some work today.

"You go ahead. I'm seeing Missy later."

Terrence zipped out of the apartment and I went to my office. There were a few messages that I needed to deal with and some paperwork that needed my signature, but it was pretty quiet. Many people were still celebrating the holiday it seemed which was kind of a relief. I had a great deal on my mind to sift through.

I was staring at a spreadsheet for heaven's knew how long when I heard a knock at the door.

"Are you busy?"

It was Jack and I welcomed the interruption.

"I can take a break. Come on in."

He settled into a chair opposite me. "I came to let you know that the background check on the Cambridges came back. They're legit collectors and while they don't have the most stellar reputations personally, professionally they're well-respected."

"What does that mean? They aren't suspects anymore?"

He sat back in the chair and shrugged. "They allowed us to search their rooms and vehicle. We didn't find anything. I also doubt that they'd want to endanger their professional reputations so they could steal the diaries. I could be wrong on that, but my gut is telling me they're not the ones. I wanted to let you know so that you wouldn't be concerned when they check out this afternoon."

Yesterday the Cambridges had asked for a late checkout, which I was happy to grant as I didn't want them leaving too soon.

"You're disappointed."

I couldn't deny it. I'm sure my feelings were written all over my face. Unlike Jack, I wasn't a pro at hiding my emotions.

"I guess I am. I was hoping it was the Cambridges."

"Because that would have made it easy. An out-of-towner

that you already don't think much of." Jack nodded in under-standing. "It rarely works out that way, though. But look on the bright side...it still could be a tourist."

"So what do you do now?"

"I wait for my friend to enhance the video from the security cameras. I'm hoping to hear from him today but it might be tomorrow."

"Do you think Natalie Martin stole the diaries? Tell me the truth, Jack. Do you really think she did it? What's that famous cop gut telling you?"

For a minute I thought he wasn't going to answer. He was giving me that enigmatic look that he loves so much and I hate, but then he finally spoke.

"No, I don't think that she did it. Because if she did, then they wouldn't be on display for the whole town anymore. That's important to her. Public recognition. If she steals them, then only she can see them. That's not what she wants." He leaned forward then, his elbows resting on the edge of my desk. "And before you ask the next obvious question, no, I don't think Iris Martin stole them, either. I don't think any of the Farradays had anything to do with this. I've talked to dozens of people since Saturday night and my personal opinion is that it's an out-of-towner. Someone who was smart enough to stay under the radar and not make him or herself known to anyone."

"That doesn't narrow it down very well."

"It doesn't. Let's hope that my friend can fix that video. Otherwise, I'm out of clues."

It wasn't like Jack to give up. Someone had taken those diaries from the civic center. Would they eventually tip their hand?

Only time would tell.

And we might not have much of that, either.

Chapter Nine

FOR THE SECOND time that day I tromped in the freezing cold, only this time I was not only with my mother, but Missy and Daisy, too. We were going to do the spells as best we could and just hope that they worked. If not, we were out of options.

The sun had gone down and the sky was cloudy – just as predicted by the weatherman – which had dropped the temperature even more, and my teeth were chattering despite a layer of thermal underwear and wool socks. My ears were numbed and my lips had to be bright blue. Missy, of course, looked like she was standing on a tropical beach sipping a margarita. My mom didn't appear all that cold, either. Luckily, Daisy was more like me and she was grumbling about the weather as well.

"See?" I said, nodding toward Daisy who was rewrapping her scarf around her neck and covering her mouth and nose. "It's cold out here. It's not just me."

"It is cold," my mother agreed. "But it's not freezing. You'll be fine. We're going to be building a bonfire. You'll be toasty warm."

If we ever got to our destination. For some reason, it felt like the walk there was twice as long as this morning. Which couldn't be the case but it felt like it.

We finally arrived at the clearing and dumped all of our supplies on the ground with a relieved and collective groan. I'd been tasked with carrying the bowl, ink, and mirror and I'd been terrified the entire way that I was going to trip in the dark and break the mirror. We needed seven years of bad luck like a hole in our heads, and it would be all my fault.

Missy and my mother immediately took charge, setting up the supplies while Daisy and I built a bonfire. I really didn't know what I was doing, but Daisy had spent years camping out with her sister when they were on the road with The Grateful Dead so she quickly had a fire built, the heat from the flames seeping into my cold bones.

The clouds were overhead. The trees quiet. The pond still. The stones of the fireplace were smooth from years of inclement weather. Everything was as it should be. Time to get this show on the road.

We sat in a circle holding hands, the bowl of red ink in the center and the mirror floating on the surface. Missy closed her eyes and chanted a few words that I didn't understand. The shiny surface of the mirror rippled in response and I watched mesmerized as a series of cracks appeared radiating out from the center. The sky lit up with one lone lightning bolt and then everything went dark and quiet again.

Missy placed a small wooden bowl in front of her and put in

the dried chamomile flowers, a sliver of raw chicken, the powdered ginger, the tree bark, the petal of a rose, and a few drops of peppermint oil. As soon as the drops hit the bottom of the bowl I could feel a change in the atmosphere around me. There was no wind but I could sense the shift in the air, almost physically lifting me from my seat.

I felt pressure on my abdomen and then the mirror sparked to life, the cracks mending before my eyes. Light emanated from the mirror and more sparks blew from the surface like a sparkler on the Fourth of July. The pond next to us bubbled and fizzed, steam rising from its depths. The pressure built until it was almost unbearably painful. I could barely breathe, and eventually spots appeared in front of my eyes and the world began to spin and tilt.

Sadly, it ended just as quickly and the mirror went dark, the bonfire extinguishing itself as if gallons of water had been thrown on it all at once. We sat there for a long time waiting for something – anything – else to happen but I could tell that the spell was over. It was just me sitting on the cold ground again. No atmospheric shift. No lightning. I could breathe again. The terrible pressure was gone.

"It didn't work," Missy finally said, her tone resigned. "I'm sorry, but it didn't work."

My mother looked like she wanted to cry. I don't think I'd ever seen her expression so sad.

"Can we try again?" she asked.

Missy shook her head. "It doesn't work like that. We'd have

to get all new supplies. These have lost their power."

"We can do that," Daisy said, her gaze darting from me to Mom and then to Missy. "Isn't it worth another try?"

"I felt it," I confessed. "I thought it was going to work."

Mom and Daisy both nodded their heads in agreement but Missy was shaking her head no.

"We don't have enough power. We're not really witches and this spell takes more power than we have. I could feel something incredibly powerful pushing back at us. Grandma said that the demon would know once we'd cast the spell. He was pushing back and he's far more forceful than we are." She turned to me. "Could you feel it? Like you'd never catch your breath again?"

"That's what that was? I thought it was part of the spell."

"It was the demon trying to keep us from completing the spell. We'll never be able to win that battle."

Now I wanted to cry. Daisy and my mom were looking shaken as well.

I took a deep breath, my lungs still aching from before. "So you're saying that the demon knows we were trying to out him?"

"Yes."

"Does he or she know it was us specifically?"

"Maybe. Probably." Missy sighed. "I don't really know. It depends on the powers that they have. Different demons can have different powers inherited from their ancestors or gifted through magical objects."

"This isn't the best news," Daisy said in a massive understatement. "What do we do now?"

"We need to see my grandmother," Missy said. "Right now. I think we may have...poked the bear."

Was it a good bear or an evil bear? I had a feeling we were about to find out.

THIRTY MINUTES LATER we were huddled around the table in Missy's grandmother's kitchen eating apple pie and drinking hot chocolate. Missy had recounted our efforts to her grandma and the older woman had listened intently, not saying a word.

That made me even more nervous than I already was, which had me eating a second slice of pie. Hey, I eat when I have anxiety, plus the pie was out of this world amazing. Her grandmother was a wickedly good baker.

"So we could feel him pushing back on the spell," Missy concluded. "Does he know who we are?"

Her expression somber, Grandma shook her head. "I'm not sure. Maybe. Depends on their powers. Most likely not, though. They probably only know that someone is trying to find out their identity. It sounds like you've got yourself one heck of a demon though, to have been able to get those sorts of physical reactions from all four of you while you were casting that spell. Normally, you'd have some protection from their pushback, but from what you've described he was able to penetrate it and shut you down. It's quite remarkable, really. I wouldn't have given you that spell if I didn't think you could pull it off."

I couldn't help my next question.

"Is it good or bad that he's that powerful?"

Grandma shrugged. "If he's good, it's the best news ever. If he's bad…"

She didn't have to finish. We all knew what she was referring to. Armageddon. An apocalypse. Humanity dying out. Evil taking over the world.

"What do we do now?" my mother asked. "What's our next step?"

Grandma shook her head again. "I don't know and I wish I did. This has gone far beyond anything I've ever dealt with. I think at this point we have to take a step back and hope that good will once again win out against evil."

Give up? She wanted us to just *give up*? Skip on down the road and just hope everything worked out okay? That was quitter talk, and my mom didn't raise a quitter. If we had to it would be just her and I fighting evil.

"You may well be right," my mother – the brand-new quitter – said. "This war has been going on for centuries. We have to believe it will continue long after we're gone."

I looked at her in disbelief. She was just going to throw in the towel. This was it. She'd tried a little bit and now she was done. She must have deciphered my expression because she started talking again.

"Now, Tedi–" she began, but I wasn't listening. I was angry.

"Don't," I said, jumping up from my chair to pace the tiny space between the table and the stove. "We can't give up.

Mankind is depending on us. We have to do something. We can't let evil win."

Missy stood as well, standing right in my path so I couldn't go around her. "We're not giving up. But we're going to have to regroup. We used up plan A, B, C, and D, Tedi. You know this. We don't have any more ideas right now, and frankly, we're powerless in this battle. Didn't you feel what I felt tonight? That demon could have killed us if he wanted to. He was only toying with us, but I could feel the unleashed power that he has. We're alive because he left us alive. Maybe because he's a good demon or he's evil and he's playing with us. Either way, we're just insignificant pests to him. I can guarantee you that he or she is not afraid of us. At all."

With that good news, I fell back into my chair. We were blocked at every turn and there didn't appear to be any other path to take.

"I hate to lose. More than I like winning."

"I know, honey," my mother said. "I don't like it much, either."

"This isn't a loss," Daisy declared. "It's only a timeout. Heck, it's not even halftime yet. There's plenty more game to go. We just need a new strategy, that's all."

Grandma had been standing at the kitchen window looking out at the backyard.

"Look," she said, pointing outside. "It's the first snow of the season. That has to be a good luck sign. It's always been that way in the past."

Walking over to the window, I watched as a few snowflakes turned into dozens and then hundreds. Within minutes, the once green lawn was a sparkling white under the moon. Normally, nothing made me happier than the first snow of the year.

"We're going to find a way," I said as the fluffy flakes fell softly on the ground. "Because we don't have any other option."

I didn't know our next move but my mother was right. We'd face it together.

I wasn't alone.

Chapter Ten

I WAS STILL feeling pretty down the next morning, so I tried to cheer myself up with bacon. Lots of it. I had several strips in the kitchen of the inn and then more when I met up with Missy at the diner that morning. She'd been concerned about me when we all went home last night and I wanted her to know that I was resilient. I would be fine. I just wasn't all that happy at the moment.

"So I've been thinking," she announced when Daisy dropped off our orders. The place was slammed with people and she could only wave and leave our food as she went by. "I know you're upset about the spell last night, but none of us are giving up. We're just figuring out our next move."

I'd had all night to think about it since I'd barely slept.

"I know and I acted childishly last night. I was just...disappointed. I really thought the spell was going to work, even though you told me that it would be difficult and complex." I paused before continuing. "It was a little scary...you know...during. I felt like my insides were being squeezed in a vise."

She nodded in understanding. "Me, too. This demon has power, that's for sure. I've never felt anything like that in my entire life and I open portals to the afterworld for a living. Just know that none of us are giving up. We'll keeping working on it."

After that I did feel better and we chatted about the upcoming holidays while eating breakfast. It was then that I realized I hadn't told her about my anonymous gifts.

"I'm not sure you can include the snow last night," I said after we'd discussed all of them one by one. "From what your grandmother said that could have been a reaction to the spell we tried to cast."

"It's possible but it's still quite the coincidence, especially as it rarely snows this early in this part of the country. We're lucky to get snow at Christmas. I only remember a couple of Thanksgivings as a child where we had snow. So you don't have any clue who is sending you these gifts? Don't you kind of think it has to be Santa?"

"It can't be. He couldn't have received my letter by the time the first gift arrived."

"Maybe it's the demon," Missy laughed. "Stranger things have happened in this town."

That was true, but I doubted I was on any demon's Christmas shopping list.

"How on earth would a demon know my Christmas list?"

"Demons all have different powers. Yes, all of them have superhuman strength and speed. Incredibly high intelligence but

GRANDMA GOT RUN OVER BY A DEMON

there are other powers they can have. Maybe the demon in town somehow read all the letters in the mailbox."

"And chose mine at random? Sort of like a pay it forward thing?"

"If it's a good demon and not an evil one, it kind of makes sense."

It didn't make sense in the least.

"I've never been that lucky in my life."

"Maybe your luck is changing."

"I won't hold my breath."

We finished our breakfast and Missy had to run an errand, so I stayed in the booth for a few minutes more answering a few texts on my phone. I was so engrossed in what I was doing, I startled when Jack slid in the same spot Missy had vacated only a few minutes before.

"Tedi."

"Jack."

"Came in for a bite of breakfast. I see that you've already eaten, otherwise I'd invite you to join me."

Putting my phone down, I gave Jack all of my attention. I wanted to hear about the video.

"I ate with Missy earlier, but I'm glad that you're here."

He gave a goofy fake grin that was frankly a little disturbing. A little like a crazed game show host. Shudder.

"Because of my sparkling personality?"

"No, because I wanted to know if you've heard from your friend about the video. Was he able to lighten it so you could see

97

who the thieves were?"

His smile dropped. "I did and I'm afraid it's not good news. He wasn't able to do anything to make it better."

My optimism was taking a battering the last twenty-four hours. I'd had high hopes.

"What's your next step?"

He shifted on the seat, looking uncomfortable, which wasn't the usual Jack Garrett that I'd come to know.

"I don't think there's much more that can be done."

Say…what?

"I don't think that I'm following you. There's nothing you can do?"

"Not at the moment," he sighed. "Not every case gets solved, Tedi. I'd love it to be that way, but the reality is that sometimes we don't find out the answers."

"So that's it? You've just given up?"

I didn't think Jack of all people would do this. He was constantly pushing and now he'd decided to stand still. Today of all days? I couldn't have been more shocked about his behavior if he'd slapped me upside the head with a two by four.

"I haven't given up," he corrected. His tone was gentle but I could tell that he didn't like explaining himself to me. He didn't like doing it with anyone. "I only have so many resources, and as the sheriff I have to make judgment calls about where to spend those resources. Right now, we have no viable leads as to where the diaries are. If a lead comes up, I'll be the first one to go after it."

"Oh."

Sighing, he started to reach out for my hand and then pulled his arm back.

"I can't win them all. I can only hope that I win the really big, important ones, Tedi."

"I know. I'm just...sad about it. The diaries mean so much to Ravenmist."

Jack didn't say anything else as the waitress dropped off a cup of coffee and took his order. When she left, I still wasn't sure what to say. This was uncharted territory. For some reason, I'd set Jack up in my mind as someone who always won. He was, however, only human. We all were and it was beginning to dawn on me that I needed to cut him – and everyone else – some slack. We were all just trying to do our best, and me being pouty about it all wasn't helping in the least. I needed a hefty dose of that optimism I was having so much trouble with.

"Tedi, are you with me? You sort of zoned out there for a minute."

I blinked a few times and shook my head. "Sorry, I was lost in thought for a moment."

"Are you mad at me?"

He didn't look all that perturbed about it if I was.

"No, I appreciate your honesty. I realize that you can't solve every case. That would be unrealistic."

Optimism. Optimism. Why was it so hard for me? Why did I struggle to see the bright side? Was it a genetic thing? My parents always seemed happy. Our home was happy growing up.

Nothing dark or sinister ever happened, and I wasn't some sort of victim. But somehow, I always expected the worst to happen. Clearly, I had issues that went far beyond diaries and demons.

What was the most optimistic thing that I could do? I needed to shake myself up a little bit.

"Jack, would you like to have dinner with me tonight?"

I've never actually seen a deer in headlights before but I would imagine that Jack's face at the particular moment looked exactly the same.

Exactly. The. Same.

"Tedi…it's complicated."

I waited for him to go on but for once he'd run out of steam. The man that was always so sure of himself had nothing to say. I didn't need him to draw me a map. I wasn't the sharpest knife in the drawer but I could work this all out for myself. For whatever reason, he didn't want to but he didn't want to be mean and say no.

I don't know why he'd asked me out that day long ago but he'd clearly changed his mind about me since then. I wasn't a glutton for punishment, and I didn't want to force him to do something that he didn't want to do.

Only willing volunteers here, folks. I take no prisoners. Dinner with me shouldn't be something that is *endured*.

"Never mind," I said, hastily standing and gathering my coat, scarf, and purse. I'd try out my optimism another time. With another human being. "I can see that you have other plans."

"Tedi, wait a minute."

He'd asked, so I did. I'd already shrugged on my coat and slung my purse over my shoulder.

I was waiting but not for much longer. Because as much as Jack had asked me to wait, he wasn't saying anything. Nothing.

He stood as well, towering over me. Honestly, he looked exhausted and I wanted to say something sympathetic to him, but he wasn't the type of guy who did sympathy. I sure didn't want any from him, either.

Picking up my phone, I tucked it into my pocket along with my scarf.

"I really need to go. See you later."

He didn't stop me as I scuttled out the door and I didn't look back over my shoulder. I'd tried and it hadn't worked out. If Missy were here, she'd tell me that it was a triumph that I'd done something optimistic but she was a lot like my mother.

You're already a winner to me, dear.

A walk in the cold air was just what a person needed to get over a bit of humiliation. There was nothing like freezing your fingers off to make one truly appreciate life. It also made me think mean thoughts about Jack being cold, too. I sorta kinda wanted his car heater to go on the blink. Not forever, mind you, just for today. Maybe tomorrow, too.

I was once again lost in my own thoughts when I felt a strong grip on my coat sleeve pulling me backward. Instinctively, I struck out with my arm and whirled around to find the handsome man from the day before standing there. He'd grabbed me.

"What are you doing? Let go of me."

His hand fell at once but he nodded toward the traffic light. "I was only trying to keep you from walking in front of a car. It says *Don't Walk*. You were going against the light."

One look confirmed his words. Darn it. I was so out of it I'd almost become road pizza.

"Gosh, I'm sorry. I didn't even realize it."

He smiled and waved away my apologies. "No harm done. You're in one piece and that's the important fact. I am glad that I ran into you. I wanted to thank you again for your kind assistance yesterday. I did have the turkey and it was as delicious as you promised. I was heading there again for breakfast."

"Waffles. Try the blueberry waffles."

"They sound delicious. I don't suppose you'd care to join me?"

After my smackdown this morning I wasn't prepared for another man to ask me to share a meal. He took my hesitation for what it was…hesitation. I didn't even know his name, for heaven's sake. Only that he was gorgeous and that he had the most amazing green eyes I'd ever seen in my life. Emerald green and bright.

"How silly of me. You don't even know my name. I'm Elijah Smith, and I swear I'm completely harmless." He smiled charmingly and held up his hands in a surrender motion. "And you are?"

Did I want to give him my name? I wasn't a standoffish

person. As the owner of an inn, I met new people every day of my life pretty much so it wasn't a big deal. The chances of him being a serial killer were low but he might be a creep.

"Tedi," I finally replied. "Tedi Hamilton. I own The Ravenmist Inn."

I said that last part because I hadn't seen him in my inn, and it was basically the only place to stay in town if you were a tourist.

"I saw that building when I was walking around. Beautifully restored. I'm staying in Marcola for a few days visiting family. I have a cousin that goes to the university. He's in classes most of the day so I've had to find ways to entertain myself."

Marcola was only thirty minutes away and the biggest city in our part of Illinois. It had a huge university there and half of the population during the school year were students.

"You should try Beckmore then if you like architecture and antiques. It's about forty-five minutes from here. They have a lovely Italian restaurant that overlooks a canal. Roberto's."

"I'll have to try that. Thank you again. You certainly know your way around this area. Have you lived here all of your life?"

"Most of it. I've also lived in Chicago."

He stroked his chin and then coughed slightly. "Listen, I'm going to go out on a limb here. I swear that I'm a nice guy and totally harmless. I don't suppose you'd agree to have dinner with me tonight? You can drive yourself if you're uncertain and keep your phone out on the table to text your friends at regular intervals. Let them know where you are at all times. What do you say? I was thinking about trying the steak place on the edge of town."

I liked the steak place, although I didn't go there very often. It was sort of dressy and I liked to be casual most of the time. Normally, I wouldn't be tempted to go anywhere with some guy I barely knew but I'd just received a huge smackdown from Jack and my ego was smarting. That's really my only excuse for what came out of my mouth next.

That and…optimism.

"Sure, yes. I'll have dinner with you." I wasn't completely crazy, though. "And I will meet you there. What time?"

His green eyes lit up. "Seven? Is that too late? Or too early? It's up to you."

"Seven is fine. I'll see you then."

We bid goodbye and I walked back to the inn, looking over my shoulder once or twice like the last time, but as before he'd already turned a corner or gone another way.

I'd said yes. I was stepping out of my comfort zone and going on a date. The first since I'd been divorced.

It was monumental. But the real question? Was it a monumental *mistake*?

Chapter Eleven

I'M GUESSING YOU can imagine how it went after that. I called Missy to let her know what had happened after she left the diner. She told Daisy, who immediately called my mom. It was a whirlwind of calls and texts after that which I eventually decided that I would stop answering. If they wanted any sort of information, they were going to have to come in person to get it.

By midafternoon even Tina at the front desk knew that I was going on my first official date since my divorce. What can I say? Gossip in a small town has a life of its own. I usually tried to never be the subject of talk in Ravenmist, and it was now that I remembered why. The story had completely been blown out of proportion. Tina had told me that she'd heard that I was going on a date with a billionaire who had a jet.

For all I knew, Elijah Smith was going to stick me with the dinner check. Order the lobster and a bottle of wine, then excuse himself to the men's room and never come back.

No, that hadn't happened to me before but I'd had some strange dates in my life. Like the time a guy's wife showed up at our table in the restaurant. Not to scream or rage. Just to ask when he planned to be home. That's it. Whatever they had going on in their marriage I wanted no part of. I feigned a headache and managed to get home before nine.

There was also this guy in college who lived in an old house on campus with three other guys. It made "Animal House" look clean and civilized. They didn't even have any actual living room furniture, just some lawn chairs. They did have a giant television though, and it played sports twenty-four-seven. He was a nice guy but after seeing the filth he lived in I just couldn't date him anymore. I kept visualizing the fuzzy kitchen and it made me nauseous.

Needless to say, I didn't have high hopes for my evening. That probably kicks me out of the Optimist Hall of Fame but I hadn't had a great deal of luck when dating.

Which was why all the females in my life felt it was their duty to come over and help me get ready. Scratch that. They wanted to come over and tell me all the reasons this was a bad idea. As if I didn't know that already. Several times during the day I'd talked myself out of going, but then I remembered that I only knew Elijah's name but not his phone number. I couldn't call him to back out, so I'd have to suck it up and perhaps actually have a nice evening out of the house. Not wearing my pajamas and not watching old movies or cooking shows.

"You should wear this."

Missy was standing in my walk-in closet, perusing my clothes. She and I didn't have the same tastes. While I preferred solid colors and tailored styles, she loved anything floaty with flowers. I look terrible in flowered material.

So what does she pull out of the closet? A flowered dress with a floaty skirt. The only reason I even had it was because she'd talked me into buying it a few years ago saying that I looked "terrific" in it.

Spoiler alert. I didn't. I looked like a flowery, unmade bed.

"I look awful in that. You should take it home for yourself. It's more your style."

Missy slid it off the hanger and held it up in front of her while looking in my full-length mirror. "It's really nice. Are you sure?"

She didn't even remember that she'd picked it out originally.

"It's all yours."

Daisy was sitting on the end of my bed and my mother was perched on a chair next to it. Did I mention that both of them were wearing disapproving expressions? You would have thought I was planning to go out and kick puppies from the way there were acting.

"Not that anyone asked my opinion, but I think this is a very bad idea, Tedi," Daisy said. "You know I'm a little psychic and the hairs on my arms are standing up at the idea of you going on this date. I don't think it's wise." She held out her arm for my inspection. "See? You need to call this off."

"I cannot call it off. I already explained that I don't have his number."

"That's the best reason for why you shouldn't go." It was my mother speaking this time. "You don't even know this man."

"That's what dating is for," I reminded her, slipping a black dress off of the hanger. "To get to know people. And you've been bugging me to go out on a date for...forever, practically. So I finally say yes and now it's a terrible idea."

"I wanted you to go out on a date with the sheriff," she said.

"Well, he didn't want to go out on a date with me," I shot back. "I asked him–"

Immediately I realized that I'd gone too far, said too much. I closed my mouth, locked it, and threw away the key.

It wasn't going to be that easy, however.

Missy's eyes were round with surprise. "Did you ask him out on a date? Oh my, and he said no?"

"I could think of about a dozen things I'd rather be doing right now than discussing this," I declared defensively. "A root canal. A colonoscopy. Having my nails pulled out with pliers comes to mind. I'm sorry I said anything. It's no one's business but mine."

My mother wasn't the best listener in the world, and she wasn't going to let this go. I already knew it, and I could see the anger rising in her red cheeks. She was mad.

"You asked Jack Garrett out and he said no? Who does he think he is? He'd be lucky to go out on a date with you. You're a wonderful woman. Smart and successful. Funny and mostly easy to be around. Obviously, he has something wrong with him. Something deeply troubling about his personality that he's been hiding from us."

Mostly easy? Thanks, Mom.

As much as Jack wasn't my favorite person at the moment, I couldn't let him be talked about negatively. It wasn't his fault that he didn't want to have dinner with me. Maybe he wasn't hungry.

"Jack doesn't have any troubling personality issues. At least that we don't already know about, Mom. He just didn't want to go out with me. That's all. No major conspiracy here."

Mom was still grumbling to herself though. Heaven help Jack if he pulled her over for speeding any time in the near future in that red sports car of hers. He was going to get an earful and he'd have no idea why.

"I don't understand," Daisy said. "Did he ask you out or did you ask him out? From what Missy said, it sounded like he asked you out but now I'm not sure. This is confusing."

Imagine how I felt.

"He asked me out first, back in May," I replied with a put-upon sigh. Couldn't we change the subject or something? "Then he got called to Chicago so we had to put it off. When he came back, he never said anything and I didn't either. Then this morning I decided to be an optimist—"

"Good for you," Missy cheered.

"Thank you. Anyway, I decided to be an optimist and I asked him if he wanted to have dinner with me tonight. He said no. And that it was complicated. Or complex. I'm not really sure exactly what he did say because he didn't say much. But I got the gist. He'd changed his mind, which is fine. I'm okay with it and we can just be friends, which was all we were anyway. In fact, nothing has changed at all."

No one said anything for a few minutes while I sorted through my wardrobe again. The black dress was really the best option.

"I think I'm going to wear this."

"You'll look beautiful in that, sweetheart," my mom said. "Very classic."

"Elegant," Daisy agreed. "Are you going to pair that with some black pumps?"

I looked at Missy. She hadn't said anything. "Well?"

She held up the flowered dress. "I still vote for this."

"I'm wearing the black."

Daisy and my mother exchanged a glance and they weren't even sly about it.

"What? Go ahead and say it."

"It's a bad idea," Daisy insisted. "I don't have a good feeling about this."

"You don't have to go," my mother argued. "You can call the restaurant and they can give him a message."

It was already five-thirty. "It's too late to cancel. I have to go. It will be fine. It's just dinner. Heck, I'll probably be home before ten. With a doggy bag. It's no big deal."

I was going to keep telling myself that until I believed it.

It was one date. How badly could it go?

I COULDN'T QUITE put my finger on why I wasn't having a good time at dinner with Elijah. He was certainly charming and witty. Funny, but not too funny, if you know what I mean. He was intelligent and well-traveled. There didn't seem to be a subject he didn't know something about, and he didn't monopolize the conversation or try to impress me with how worldly and wise he was.

He asked me quite a bit about myself and by the time I'd almost finished my starter salad and half of my entrée, I'd realized that he'd managed to find out a great deal about my childhood.

But I hadn't found out much about him. He'd answered my questions but never in a specific way. It was always rather vague, like his childhood years were happy and his parents were wonderful. He'd done well in school but he wasn't a brainiac. He didn't like sports and he liked books better, but I couldn't have told you what books he liked at all. Somehow, he'd changed the subject before I could find out.

The food was good, the service excellent. My dinner companion was pleasant and heck, even the restaurant wasn't too cold or too hot. It was so annoyingly...perfect.

And I didn't feel any sort of spark for this guy. He could have been any one of a hundred million people that I'd been randomly sat with to share this meal. That's how it felt.

"I hope you saved room for dessert," he said with a smile. "I'm told they have an excellent chocolate mousse."

Honestly, I wasn't sure I wanted to extend the evening with

him long enough to wolf down some creamy mousse that was, as he'd said, to die for. This wasn't working. It wasn't his fault. It was mostly me. I didn't want to be here anymore, and this had been a mistake. Nothing bad had happened as Daisy had predicted, but this hadn't been my best idea ever. I was already planning to offer to pick up half of the check, thank him for a nice time, and drive home. I'd put my pajamas on, make some hot chocolate and watch television with Terrence.

I was about to tell him that I wasn't hungry for dessert when a high-pitched buzzer interrupted any flow of thought I might have had. It buzzed over and over, loud enough to crack glass and I had to place my hands over my ears to get any relief at all. The maître'd ran over to our part of the dining room and made a swooping motion toward the door with his arms.

"Fire alarm!" he yelled, his hair almost standing on end and his eyes wide with fear. "Everyone evacuate immediately."

Did I mention that I have bad luck on dates? I know what you're thinking. That this is just a continuation of that, but I was so thrilled that the date was being abruptly ended that I happily grabbed my purse and coat and jogged out of the restaurant in my high heels. If I played my cards right, I could be home and in my pajamas in less than thirty minutes.

Elijah, on the other hand, was less than pleased about the turn of events. He was frowning while trying to be upbeat and smiling.

"There's a wine bar—"

No, no, no. No wine bar. No extending this torture. I was

done.

"I can't really," I said, interrupting him. I wanted to be polite but I also needed to be firm as well. "It's been a lovely evening but I think I should head home. You probably should, too."

We'd been corralled out in the far reaches of the parking lot while the fire department pulled their trucks up close to the building. I'd parked out here anyway as I was persnickety about door dings. I didn't know where Elijah had parked.

Luckily, he didn't push, which was a relief.

"You worked all day. I'm sure you're tired," he replied, pulling out his phone for a moment and checking it. "I'll be going home soon but perhaps I'll see you at The Grateful Raven tomorrow."

"That's a possibility."

But not a big one.

He pointed to the far side of the restaurant. "I parked over there. So…"

Yes…so…right.

"Thank you again," I said. "The meal was lovely."

"It was." He frowned again and his gaze quickly ran over the crowd that was dispersing rapidly. "I suppose I can call them tomorrow and settle our bill."

I automatically reached for my purse. "Let me–"

"No, it was my treat. You were my guest. I'm happy to get it."

"Thank you," I said again. "That's very nice."

"So…"

"So…"

There wasn't much more to say, and he seemed to get that. I thought for a moment he wanted to shake my hand or maybe hug. I wasn't down for that but he didn't end up moving closer to me, instead taking a few steps back and giving me a cheery wave before disappearing around the corner of the building.

Thank goodness that was over.

The fire department had two trucks, but I didn't see any smoke at all from the roof or any windows. Hopefully, it was simply a small kitchen fire and they had it under control.

My car was a few rows away and I dug into my purse for my keys as I walked toward it. I should have been paying more attention, but this is Ravenmist and we don't exactly have a huge crime problem. I wasn't the type to be on my guard everywhere I went.

Two steps from my vehicle, an SUV sped down the aisle and stopped right in front of me. The passenger door swung open and that was when I recognized the car and the driver.

Missy.

"Get in."

I didn't argue.

She didn't speak at first, intent on navigating her way around the fire trucks and the people still milling about in the cold. I didn't speak either, because she had this weird intense look on her face that I'd never seen before.

And I'd known her since we were five. It was kind of freaking me out.

"We're going to Hell."

Those were the first words out of Missy's mouth in the last three minutes. She'd pulled up her vehicle to the back of the inn and parked, but left the motor running.

"Probably we are, but I'm not sure what that has to do with you picking me up tonight. What's going on? Did you pull the fire alarm?"

"Yes, I had to get you out of there so we could leave."

"That's against the law."

"I'll risk it."

"So where are we going?"

"We're going to Hell," she repeated. "As in the place. Right now. Grandma talked to my uncle and he believes that the situation is dire enough for him to use his connections in the supernatural world. We're going to fly down to Florida where there's a portal to Hell that is controlled by the good guys."

Oh. What kind of travel agent booked those vacations?

"Too bad we don't know where the portal is right here in Ravenmist," I replied. "It would save us a trip."

Although Florida – and Hell – had to be a heck of a lot warmer than Illinois in the winter.

"Hopefully we'll get to talk to Lucifer, or at least one of his senior staff. He might be able to tell us who the demon is, or maybe the entrance."

Senior staff. Like a corporation. I'd love to read that mission statement.

"Maybe? He doesn't know all of the entrances?"

Kind of lame…for the devil and all.

"Some portals are created by magic. There could be literally tens of thousands all over the world. He can't keep track of them all."

"Why would he even help us? Doesn't he want the dead to rise and wipe out all of mankind?"

It sounded like just the thing that he would go for.

Missy shook her head. "Absolutely not. If the dead rise, then he has no one to rule over. Also, if mankind is wiped out, he gets no new souls. Pretty much puts him out of business. With the evil demons ruling over earth, he'll have much less power as well. My uncle thinks he might help us, although it's a huge maybe. Lucifer doesn't really like people who are alive to come down there. He says it's not good for morale."

I could see his point.

"But we're going anyway?"

"Yes, you need to change into something more comfortable to travel in. Preferably layers. It will be hot there."

An understatement, I was sure.

Next stop? Hell.

Chapter Twelve

WE WEREN'T IN Hell yet but we might as well have been. Airport security took forever and then our flight was delayed for hours. We ate a snack but we spent most of our time sitting in those hard-plastic chairs hoping that the plane would show up. When it finally did, we piled on and promptly fell asleep only to be awakened by a surly flight attendant telling us to move our seats to the upright position. We had arrived.

We hadn't checked any bags, so we deplaned quickly and headed straight for the rental car that Missy had reserved. It looked like a small, shiny roller skate, but she said she'd gotten a great deal. We shoved our carry-ons into the hatchback and headed out onto the highways.

I'd already shed my jacket and sweater and was thinking about my shirt next. It was hot. As in over eighty degrees. I loved it and hated it in equal measure. If we'd been here to sit by the pool...

But we were on a mission and that meant that we had to stay on course. No side paths to get margaritas.

"Do you know where you're going?"

Missy wasn't using any GPS tool and she didn't appear fazed in the least by the heavy traffic.

"I'm attuned to my uncle's energy."

Enough said. I trusted her supernatural abilities to get us where we were going in one piece.

It was about an hour later when she pulled into the massive driveway of a large home on a huge lot. The entire neighborhood looked incredibly fancy, far too posh for me in my old blue jeans and sneakers.

The door opened as Missy parked the car in the shade of a huge oak tree. I recognized her uncle and his wife, him dressed in his usual khaki cargo shorts and Hawaiian flowered shirt and her in a casual red sundress. Their lined skin was golden from the sun and their hair was heavily flecked with gray, but they flew down the front porch steps as if they were teenagers, grabbing Missy and giving her a huge hug.

Then they turned to me.

I'd met them several times before, but not since finding out that her uncle was *the* Grim Reaper. So it was with some trepidation that I allowed myself to be pulled into a bear hug. I was happy to find out that nothing was really different. The earth didn't shift and grasshoppers didn't take over the earth.

"We're so glad you're here," Tessa, Missy's aunt said with a huge smile. "We have your rooms all set up, and there's food on the back verandah. We thought you might want to eat and then freshen up before your trip."

To Hell.

Freshened probably wasn't how they usually received their guests.

Uncle Ralph insisted on carrying our suitcases and we followed him up a sweeping staircase. He was chattering about the weather and asking how cold it was up in Ravenmist.

"Not a fan of the cold," he said, pushing open a door on the left side of the hallway. "Tedi, this will be your room, and Missy is in the one next door. I'll leave you ladies to freshen up and meet you on the verandah. We can talk there."

My room was beautiful, all done in blue with touches of gold, with whitewashed furniture. The bed was gigantic and I had a strange urge to jump on the mattress a few times like when I was a kid.

"Hey, earth to Tedi, are you listening to me?"

No, I wasn't. I shook my head, trying to loosen the cobwebs in my brain. This was becoming a bad habit.

"I am now. Sorry, I need some coffee."

"My family will have it downstairs. How about I meet you there in ten?"

"Sounds good."

After splashing some water on my face and touching up my lipstick, I met Missy and her aunt and uncle downstairs. They were sitting outside on a covered verandah digging into a table full of food. My stomach growled loudly, complaining that I hadn't fed it in hours so I sat down and quickly filled my plate. Missy was updating her family on all the goings-on in Ravenmist, particularly the Christmas tree-lighting ceremony and the stolen diaries. Uncle Ralph and Aunt Tessa asked about Grandma and the cousins. When I was full and they'd run out of conversation, the topic turned to why we were there in the first place.

"There's a few things you need to know before you go," Uncle Ralph said, placing his fork on the edge of his plate. "First, I'm not thrilled that you're doing this but I see that we don't really have any options left. Second, I have some doubts that this is going to be successful. Luc is a difficult person and cares little for anyone but himself. He certainly has reasons to help us but sometimes he simply likes being stubborn and pigheaded. Third, *whatever you do, no matter what he says or does, do not sign anything.* Do you understand? I cannot emphasize this enough. Do not make any agreement with him for his help. He either gives his assistance freely or you walk away. You cannot trust him. Understood?"

Uncle Ralph was a little red in the face so I took the warning seriously.

"No deals with the devil," I said. "Got it. And don't trust him."

Tessa nodded. "Even if he agrees to help us we can't trust anything that he says. We'll have to check it out."

"He can also be incredibly charming and funny," Uncle Ralph said. "He can actually be a fun guy to be around. He's smart and entertaining but never let your guard down when you're around him. That's what he wants."

This was sounding worse and worse by the second.

"Are you coming with us?" Missy asked. "I have to admit that I'm nervous about this."

"Me too," I offered up, gulping down more coffee. I desperately needed it.

"I can take you to the portal but I'm not going any farther. Luc and I have a history and it's not a good one. I'm afraid that if he takes one look at me, he'll dig in his heels and never help. We have a better chance with you two. He has an eye for the ladies. Considers himself to be quite the Lothario."

The Devil might make some moves on me? For real?

A few minutes later we climbed into Uncle Ralph's BMW sedan and headed out to the portal. He'd explained that it was completely protected by the forces of good, which was a relief. Missy had told me before we left Ravenmist that if anything should happen while we were down there – such as the portal falling into evil hands – we might not be able to get back to the mortal plane. In other words, we'd be stuck. Forever. She'd said that so I could make my own decision about going.

Because it was dangerous. A fact I'd decided not to dwell on. If Uncle Ralph and Aunt Tessa were comfortable enough to let their niece go down there then I could go too. And there was no way I was letting my best friend do something this stupid and reckless alone. We were a team.

Did I mention that I'd sent one text to my mother about leaving town? A vague message about Missy and I doing some demon research and needing to go right away. I'd tell her the details when I returned. She could have a nervous breakdown when she knew I was safe and sound.

He pulled into a strip mall and parked the car in front of a laundromat. Flipping open the glove compartment, he handed Missy a folded-up piece of paper with a gold seal.

"This is your paperwork. Don't lose it. It's the only thing that will get you into to see Luc."

Missy accepted it, nodding silently. Then he dug into his pocket and pulled out two gold coins that looked ancient. He handed one to each of us.

"That's your fare. I'll wait here for you."

Uh…what? Where were we going? It was time? Thankfully, Missy appeared to know. She and her uncle must have talked about this before I came downstairs to eat. She and I exited the vehicle and I followed her into the laundromat. There were a few people there but they barely glanced at us, either staring at their phones or folding their freshly laundered towels.

Beckoning me over to the oversized washers – the kind you could wash a king-sized comforter in, she opened the last one in the row. It had an *Out of Order* sign on it.

"Okay, get in."

"Pardon?"

She pointed to the inside of the washer. "Get in. This is the entrance."

Nervously, I glanced over my shoulder at the people already in the laundromat.

"Shouldn't we wait until they're done? I mean…we don't want them to see, right?"

I kept my voice down and leaned close so Missy could hear me.

"They're soldiers of good and they're job is to protect the portal. They know why we're here."

In that case...I didn't have a good reason not to step into the washer. Except that I was slightly claustrophobic. This was a good time to get over it because the entrance to Hell was a washing machine.

Raising one leg, I stuck it inside the machine and then hesitated. "Is it like a slide down? What should I expect?"

"I have no idea."

"That's not exactly comforting."

"I didn't really mean it to be. I can go first if you want."

"No, it's fine. My...leg is already in here. It's kind of small, that's all." I shoved my head and torso in as well. It smelled like...something familiar, but I couldn't place it. That I hadn't expected. "There's a scent in here but I can't quite–"

I never got to finish my sentence. I was pulled into the washer by a powerful force, sucking the oxygen from my lungs. It didn't feel like when we'd cast the spell. It was...more and different. It felt like I was falling into a giant pool of liquid and I couldn't crawl up to the top to catch my breath.

I was sure we'd made a lethal mistake.

Chapter Thirteen

A S QUICKLY AS I'd been sucked into the washer, I was
suddenly standing next to Missy in an elevator all made of
chrome, listening to bad instrumental music. So this was the
elevator to Hell? It reminded me of a snooty department store in
downtown Chicago. And it smelled...like summer.

The doors slid open and we stepped out and into what
looked like a standard cosmetics department. In fact, it looked
exactly like Simpson's in Ravenmist. And I do mean *exactly*.

"Are you seeing what I'm seeing?"

Missy nodded, her gaze darting from one corner of the room
to the other. "It's Simpson's. Isn't it?"

"It looks like it."

"But it can't be. I mean...we're in Hell."

At least we should be.

"Is there some way that the dryer we took could have delivered us back home?"

"I don't think so. That would be weird."

Because visiting Hell wasn't strange enough on its own.

I looked over my shoulder and the elevator that we'd taken

had disappeared and there was only a blank wall. That decided it then. There was no way to go but forward.

"The elevator is gone," I informed Missy. "There's no way back."

"Uncle Ralph warned me that we might encounter some out of the ordinary things. I guess this is one of them. Shall we?"

"We shall."

Linking arms, we stepped forward into the aisles. The store appeared to have several customers but they didn't pay any attention to us. I was studying an older woman looking at lipsticks when, out of nowhere, I was sprayed with liquid right in the face.

Coughing and gagging, I turned to find a smiling woman holding up an ornate bottle.

"It's *Nuit de Lucifer.* Just ten thousand dollars an ounce."

"I'll pass," I choked out, waving her off. Missy had been sprayed as well with some other toxin, but we managed to stumble out of the cosmetics department and into women's wear. My eye was immediately drawn to an emerald green dress that was amazing. Wait, not just amazing, but scintillating. It was every dream come true. I dropped Missy's arm and practically ran over to it. It had to be mine.

I flipped through the rack once, and then twice. They had every size but mine. What the heck?

"I can't find my size," Missy moaned from a few feet away. She was also pawing through a rack of red dresses that would have looked gorgeous on her. "My size isn't here at all. Anywhere."

Checking other racks of clothing, I confirmed what my best friend was saying. There was nothing that we could wear. Beautiful clothing, but none of it was for us.

Yep, this was Hell.

"I don't think it's a coincidence that neither of us can find our size," I finally said, giving up with a sigh. "I don't think I want to shop here anymore."

"Me, neither. Uncle Ralph said to check in at the front gate. Let's see if we can find it."

We walked along the brightly lit aisles, the tempting wares almost too much to resist, but somehow we managed to ignore them. We stepped out of the front entrance into what looked like a mall. Missy elbowed me in the ribs and pointed to a sign on the front of the store we'd just left.

Hellgate Department Store. Open every day.

"Well, we're definitely in Hell."

"We are," Missy replied, her expression morphing into a frown. "Um, Tedi. Was that there a second ago?"

Turning to see what she was looking at, a store entrance had appeared across the hallway with a giant neon sign over the top and balloons of every color around the opening.

Entrance to Hell.

"We're here," I said in a creepy sing-song voice. "Do you have that paperwork?"

She patted her purse. "I do. Are you ready?"

"No, but let's do this anyway."

There was no turning around and going back.

WE WERE WAITING in the longest line I'd ever seen in my life. It was like something out of an amusement park, twisting and winding toward our ultimate goal, but it was taking forever to get there. I kept checking the digital clock on the wall and it said we'd only been there for twenty minutes but I swear it felt like all day.

The room was warm, too. It hadn't been all that hot in the department store but here in line the temperature was definitely higher. My sweater was tied around my waist, but I was still sweating slightly.

"It seems like this line is taking forever," the man in front of me sighed. He turned around and I froze. He had a nasty hole in his forehead. "I hope we get moving soon."

Missy didn't appear bothered in the least but she was the grim reaper. "How long have you been waiting?"

He glanced at the clock on the wall and then stroked his chin. "About four days, I think. Maybe five. Time goes fuzzy when you're dead. I can't wait to get my paperwork and find out how I died. I don't remember a thing."

Uh...dude...I think you were shot.

The line began to move again and he didn't say anything to us after that, chatting to the woman in front of him. Eventually we arrived at the front of the line and a man in a black shirt and tie sat behind a large oak desk, busily typing on a laptop. He didn't even look up, just held out his hand.

"Papers?"

Missy quickly retrieved our papers from her purse and handed them over. He read through them and then heaved a huge sigh.

"This is not the right line," he said, finally looking up and giving us a scowl. "You're not dead. This is the line for processing the dead. You want the visitors line. Over there."

Holy moly, that line was worse than the one we'd just waited in. We'd be here until I was sixty.

"But we've waited so long in this line," Missy protested. "Can't you help us?"

His lips firmed into a thin line. "We have regulations and processes here for a reason. The process is the process and we can't just ignore the process. Following the process is crucial."

Hail to the process! It sounded just like...

Heavens to Mergatroid. It sounded like my evil corporate job back in Chicago. Now that was Hell.

Without any choice, we shuffled over to the other line, which luckily was moving much faster than the last one. When we got to the front the woman at the desk took one look at our papers and nodded.

Whew. Thank goodness we were in the right place this time.

"We need to get you through security," she said, reaching into a drawer and pulling out a stack of paper. "You'll need to fill out these forms and then go down that hall there to the security office so they can take your picture and issue you a visitor's badge."

More processes. Of course.

"This is a nightmare," I hissed to Missy as we sat and filled out various forms that all asked for the same information. "It's like being back at my corporate job."

"We *are* in Hell," she reminded me. "I don't think we're supposed to be enjoying our trip."

Fifteen forms later we marched down the hall to the security office and had two horrible photos taken. The image of me was so bad it made my driver's license look like a shot of a super-model. I was barely recognizable.

The guard in uniform handed Missy her badge. "Turn right at the end of the hall and follow the red line until you get to the boss's office. Good luck."

We were going to need it.

The building was a labyrinth of corridors that seemingly went nowhere. Some hallways didn't even have any doors; they just went on and on. We'd worked up a sweat by the time we reached the end of the red line. Right in front of a large set of wooden double doors with gold lettering.

Lucifer, CEO

Hell, Incorporated

My stomach had slowly been tightening into a knot with every step we'd taken since getting our badges and that little voice in my head was questioning whether this was a good idea. Too late. Missy twisted the gold doorknob and we stepped into

Satan's waiting room.

Plush. Lucifer was clearly pulling in the big bucks. Everything was gold and the carpet was so thick I swear my shoes sank about three inches into it. The office had the faint smell of money and…the beach.

"Can I help you?"

The older woman behind the reception desk appeared annoyed at our arrival. She was dressed all in red, including her hair and nails.

Missy held out the papers she'd been given by her uncle. "Hello, my name is Missy and this is Tedi. We're here–"

"We know why you're here. We've been expecting you. You've certainly taken your time getting here," she scolded. "He hasn't eaten lunch yet because he was waiting."

He? I knew who she meant.

"We tried to get here earlier," I defended. "But the line was so long and there were all these forms–"

"It's the process," she snapped, her head swiveling so she could look directly at me. "And the process is the process. You have to respect it."

"I will."

What else could I say? They were sticklers for the *process*.

She handed Missy back her papers. "Your fare, please?"

The gold coins we'd been given. We dug them out of our pockets and held them out. The receptionist sighed and rolled her eyes.

"We don't take cash anymore. Haven't for years. We don't

take personal checks, either. Credit cards only. We're completely digital. I can give you a copy of our privacy policy. Your data is safe with us."

Would my Amex work in Hell? Just what would the transaction on my statement say?

Then we heard a buzzing sound and the woman's fingers came up to her ear. She was listening to someone that wasn't us.

"Fine, we'll take the coins." She collected them and then nodded to a door behind her. "He's waiting for you through there."

Finally. We were going to talk to Satan.

Just another day in my humdrum life.

SATAN LOOKED LIKE a surfer dude. A cross between Brad Pitt and a young Robert Redford, only in board shorts and flip flops. With zinc oxide sunscreen on his nose.

I'd imagined his office as formal with lots of dark oak but no, it was a cabana on the beach. The scent of coconuts and salt hung in the air. Now I knew where that smell was coming from.

He was sitting in a lounge chair and sipping on an umbrella drink. He beckoned us to have a seat on the other two chairs.

Alrighty then. We were well down the rabbit hole. This entire trip had been surreal. Any moment I expected someone to jump out from around a corner and tell me I was being punked.

However, I had a suspicion that all this tropical wonderfulness was just a smoke screen. Beaches and warmth always relaxed me, but today I was on high alert. Lucifer wasn't going to sneak by me when I wasn't paying any attention and staring at the waves on the beach instead.

Note to self. Stop looking at the waves on the beach and sniffing the coconut sunscreen.

"Are you thirsty? These rum drinks are wonderful. I highly recommend."

Uncle Ralph hadn't mentioned whether we should accept an offer of food or drink from the devil, but I had a sneaking suspicion it wasn't a good idea. Wasn't there a myth about Persephone eating some pomegranate seeds or something? It was so hot I would have loved to have a cool drink, though.

"No, thank you," Missy said primly, sending me a warning look. I guess the rum was out of the question. "I'm assuming you know why we're here."

"I do, and I'm surprised your uncle let you come all by yourself. I would have thought he'd accompany you."

The sound of the water sliding against the sand was calm and tranquil, but the mood inside the bright blue cabana was anything but. Missy's lips pressed together and she lifted her chin in defiance.

"You know why he's not here."

"I know everything. I know things that are yet unknown."

Oh goody. He liked to talk like a bad B-movie. I'd been uncharacteristically quiet this entire trip but I was barely hanging on here, wanting to ask questions. I didn't say it out loud, though, somehow I must have captured his attention. His gaze swung from Missy to me, his blue-silver gaze intense. For a second they became mere slits, like the eyes on a rattlesnake.

"Hello, Tedi. What is it that you want to say?"

Missy's eyes went round as if she was terrified I was going to insult his clothes, which was ridiculous. I loved casualwear.

"We need your help."

"And I want to give it," Lucifer replied promptly. "What do you need from me?"

"The battle between good and evil," Missy said. "Ravenmist will be caught in the middle. A demon has brought massive amounts of supernatural energy to our town. We need to know who it is."

He smiled, but it wasn't a friendly one. "If I tell you, what will you do? They're a demon, more powerful than you can even comprehend."

"If he's a good demon, we want to talk to him," I explained. "We might be able to help him."

That seemed to amuse Satan. "You think you could help a demon? I doubt he needs your assistance."

Grasping, I glommed onto his words and wouldn't let go. "You said *he*. Is it a male?"

"Don't take my pronouns as any telltale sign," he scoffed. "But I stand by my statement. How on earth could you help a demon? You're human and weak. Besides, this battle has been waged for millennia. Do you honestly think that you can stop it? That's absurd."

I didn't like this guy. Not one bit.

"People will die," I said desperately. "Evil could wipe out all humankind. That wouldn't be good for you."

He seemed to consider my words. "True. That wouldn't be ideal, but I'd adapt."

Missy and I exchanged a worried glance. This wasn't going well. We'd known from the beginning this was a long shot, the proverbial Hail Mary pass with one second on the clock, but deep down I'd hoped for more.

This was my last ditch effort.

"I'm sure you'd adapt…to having less power."

His gaze swung to me and his eyes were like slits again; only the blue irises had turned decidedly gold. "So the little red kitten has claws? Maybe you'd like to make a deal? I help you and you help me."

I was going to say no but Missy didn't even give me a chance. She jumped up from her chair and shook her head. "No. No deals. Help us or don't help us. That's the terms."

Lucifer looked down at his drink, rubbing the tips of his fingers together. I hadn't noticed before but his nails were yellowed and pointy. Ick.

He took another sip of his drink and then smiled. A smarmy one. Too slick. I was going to need about six showers when we were done with this meeting.

"I'll tell you what. In the interest of being sporting, I'll give you some help just to make the playing field a little more fair. It wouldn't be fun for me to watch if you were all slaughtered so easily. It's the challenge that keeps my days interesting. So I won't tell you who the demon in Ravenmist is."

Now I really didn't like him.

"But I will tell you where the portal to Hell is and how to close it. That should even the odds between your quaint little town and the great evil scourge."

Neither of us answered for a long moment. I was playing his words over and over in my mind to see if there was any trap and I assumed that Missy was doing the same. Eventually, we both nodded cautiously.

"We won't sign anything," Missy said quickly. "There will be no give and take."

Chuckling, Satan took another sip of his drink. "Of course, I'm doing this out of the goodness of my...heart."

This was some sort of trap. I was sure it was. Missy was pale and I assumed that I was as well, but neither one of us could turn this down. If we could close the portal, then at least Ravenmist wouldn't be one of the first places to be slaughtered by the risen dead. He was right. It was a fighting chance, especially if we had a good demon in our midst.

"So tell us where it is," I finally said. "And how to seal it."

In a small sort of way, we'd made a deal with the devil.

Chapter Fourteen

ISSY AND I walked out of Lucifer's office, thinking we'd be returned to his secretary, but to our shock we were standing on the outskirts of Ravenmist. Our carry-on bags were sitting on the ground next to us, our coats and gloves piled on top.

Looks like we wouldn't need that return ticket from Florida. Was Uncle Ralph still sitting in the car outside the laundromat? And what about our rental vehicle?

"Uh, that was a quick trip," Missy muttered, pulling out her cell phone from her pocket. "I need to let my uncle know that we're not coming out of that building."

Shivering, I shrugged into my coat and tugged on my gloves. "From the beach to the frozen tundra in three-point-five seconds. That's a shock to the system."

Missy frowned, pausing as she tapped out a text. "What do you mean the beach? We weren't at the beach."

"Lucifer's office," I reminded her. "It was a cabana at the beach. You could smell the suntan lotion and hear the seagulls."

"No, we were in a library. There were walls and walls of

books. It smelled like musty books."

It was beginning to dawn on me that Missy and I might have had two different experiences in Hell.

Hell was *personalized*.

Satan had shown us what he thought would relax and make us the most comfortable. For me, it was the beach and for Missy it was a library.

"That's not what I saw. That makes me wonder if we can trust our eyes now. Maybe we're really not in Ravenmist."

Except that it looked like it. We were standing on the side of the road just outside of town, near a hill with a big rock at the top. I'd spent many a snowy day in my childhood sledding down that hill with my friends and family.

Being kids, we'd named it the obvious thing. Big Rock Hill. Hey, I never said we were imaginative. But if someone said Big Rock Hill, everyone knew where you were talking about.

Missy pointed to the top of the hill. "He said it was near a gathering of rocks. Do you think that's it?"

"Could be, but I honestly don't remember there being a gathering of rocks at the top of the hill. I only remember the one big one."

"Have you ever been here when there wasn't snow on the ground? It could be covering them up."

Had I? I cast back in my memory but nothing popped up. When it wasn't snowy and slippery, athletic in-shape people would run up the hill because it was healthy. That sounded painful in the knees to me and I'd avoided doing it at all costs.

"I don't think I have. I guess it's worth checking out. But we'll have to come back because we don't have the supplies we need."

Missy held up a tiny sack. "He's thought of everything. This was sitting next to my bag. I think it has what we need."

She unzipped it and held it open. Two items. Salt and a knife. A big, scary looking one, too. My stomach lurched sickeningly at the thought of using it. Okay, I'm a wuss.

"Looks like we're going to go close a portal to Hell then," I replied, zipping up my coat a little higher and wrapping a scarf around my neck. If I was going to be out here in the cold freezing to death I might as well try to keep my ears and fingers from falling off. Even if we did manage to actually close this entrance to the underworld, we still had a long, cold walk back to town. "Are you ready?"

Missy took a deep breath and smiled. "Let's do this."

We'd been given rather vague instructions, but it was all we'd been able to wrestle out of Lucifer without making some sort of deal in return. He told us to use the stones at the site to create a pentagram, then use the salt to create a ring around the pentagram. Lastly, we needed the blood of a truly good person shed in the center of the circle. That would close the portal. Supposedly. I wasn't sure we should trust the devil to be frank. For all I knew we would be casting a spell to summon hundreds of evil demons to Ravenmist. It was a risk either way.

If we did it we could be causing even more trouble, but if we didn't, we might be passing up our only chance to seal the entrance.

Leaving our things at the base of the hill, Missy threw the small bag over her shoulder and we began trudging slowly up the steep incline. Now I'll be honest here with you…It's been a long time since I'd been sledding. College, maybe? So it's been awhile and I was younger. But I didn't remember it being this much work and taking so long to climb this hill. Halfway up I was gasping and holding my sides like I had a two-pack a day habit and spent most of my time in front of the television.

Okay, the second part was true.

I stopped and looked down the hill. We hadn't gotten far.

"I feel like we should be at the top by now."

Missy looked down too, her teeth worrying her bottom lip. "I think so, too. I think…that there's a force trying to keep us from getting to the top."

A *force*. A rather vague term but I caught her meaning.

"Like witchcraft?"

"I don't know. Maybe. I just know that we're working way too hard to climb this hill and we haven't made much progress. Someone has protected it with charms or spells."

"So that's good news, right? That means that the entrance must be at the top."

"That is good news. The bad news is that if it's protected then this task could get a heck of a lot more difficult."

Boy, did it get difficult. By the time we crested the hill, we were crawling on our hands and knees, raking the dirt with our glove-encased fingernails. I was coughing and dragging oxygen into my starved lungs and I had a stitch in my side the size of a king-sized comforter. I wanted to lie down and die right then and there but the minute we hit the top it began to storm, the icy rain pelting my bare skin painfully. Lightning lit up the sky and bolts flew down, hitting the earth randomly and far too close to us for comfort. We scrambled the last few feet to the big rock, clinging to it and trying to get some protection from the electric darts that were singeing the earth every few seconds.

"This is bad," Missy panted, her cheek pressed against the smooth rock. I'd made myself as small as possible against it as well, but it was as if we'd offended Zeus himself. "This is very bad. We need to get this portal closed as quickly as possible."

I was all for that but we could barely move.

Wiping the rain out of my eyes, I finally was able to get a good look at the big rock area. There were dozens of smaller rocks. Just as Lucifer had said. Okay, we needed to make a pentacle out of these.

Um, how do you do that?

"A pentacle is a five-pointed star, right?" I asked, beginning to gather the stones together. A bolt of lightning landed about a foot to my left. I could actually feel the hair on my head stand up in reaction.

"Yes," Missy said, making a star motion with her arms. "Just like this. Let's do this fast."

As I reached for the first stone the wind shifted and the lightning ceased, which was a relief, but it was short-lived. The air swirled around us and then the rain became even more vicious, pounding the ground with its intensity like hammers against a nail. The ground undulated underneath us like a wild bucking bronco and this animal was definitely trying to throw us off. I had to ditch my gloves, and I was holding onto the dirt by my fingernails while simultaneously trying to build a pentagram with slippery rocks. What was next? Pestilence and plague?

But we did it. The pentagram was laid out with the rocks. Missy pulled the salt container from the bag and carefully created a circle around the star, which wasn't as easy as it sounded. The minute she poured the first granule of salt it was as if she'd awoken a sleeping giant. Thunder clapped so loudly my ears rang and the rain went from icy to boiling in a split second. Every streak that ran down my bare flesh burned, leaving a bright red stripe in its wake.

Any sane person would have given up by now, but I kept reminding myself that the fate of humanity was in the balance. They were depending on us not to be complete cowards. Even though I was totally a big fraidy-cat. I don't even like camping and now here I was in a vortex of storms, being beaten up by the elements.

Her long dark hair whipping in the violent wind, Missy put the salt back into the bag and pulled out the last item. The knife. We both knew what this meant. One of us had to shed blood.

"A good person has to offer up drops of their blood," she yelled, trying to be heard over the thunder. Her face was bright red and swollen. I could barely see her eyes. "You need to cut your hand and drip the blood in the center of the star."

Me? Wait a gosh darn second. We needed a *good* person. I hardly qualified. Heck, without my coffee I was barely a human being.

"I'm not good," I screamed, the wind taking my words and slapping them back in my face, along with a rush of boiling rain. "I don't even take my own bags to the grocery store. I yell at other drivers. I'm impatient with children. I'll take the last piece of cake and not even feel guilty about it."

"I'm not much better," Missy yelled, her fingertips digging into the soft earth to hold on. Our skin was an angry red color now and welts were beginning to form on the backs of our hands. Ewww. "I yelled at my mom the other day when she was driving. I've re-gifted."

That didn't sound so bad, but my reply was swallowed up when the ground underneath my best friend in the whole world crumbled and she suddenly and swiftly slid down the hill all the way to the bottom in a mudslide of epic proportions. I'd barely even had time to react when she waved at me from where she'd come to a stop. She was okay, but there was no way she could climb back up.

I was on my own.

A huge part of me wanted to give up. My skin was boiling off, my body was sore from the beating it was taking from the rain, wind, and flying projectile branches, and I was exhausted and near the breaking point. Which I supposed was the point of whomever had placed these charms and spells here. They didn't want me to finish my task.

I couldn't let Ravenmist, Missy, and all of humanity down. It was all up to me and this was no time to be a quitter. Reaching for the knife, I braced myself for the pain before taking the point and gouging the fleshy part of my palm. Apparently, Lucifer had given us a super sharp knife because blood began to seep up immediately, crimson against the blistered skin.

Holding my palm over the center of the circle I let a few drops fall to the earth. Then held my breath.

Nothing.

I squeezed a few more drops and for a moment I thought it had worked. The rain halted but then I was pelted even harder a second later, and it wasn't rain this time.

It wasn't water coming down from the sky. It was frogs and snakes. I inwardly shuddered as a frog plopped on top of my head and then fell carelessly to the earth before hopping off to wherever frogs from the sky went. Then a snake hit me and then a frog and then a snake...

And did I mention that I *hate* snakes? I'm terrified of them. Like run for the hills frightened and here they were slithering all around me and I wanted to do nothing more than join Missy at the bottom of the hill.

What was I supposed to do now? My blood hadn't worked and now we were getting pelted by reptiles and amphibians. Missy wasn't here to advise me and it was all I could do to hold my position when the entire ground underneath me was determined to throw me off of the spinning globe and send me into orbit.

Then as quickly as the frogs and snakes began, they stopped and the ground stopped bucking and twisting. Had it worked and there was some sort of delay?

No, when I turned to look up at the sky the frogs and snakes were still falling but… It was like I had a large umbrella over me. They were falling all around but not right on me.

"Move aside, Tedi."

That wasn't Missy's voice, but it was familiar.

Jack was standing to my right and the frogs weren't hitting him, either. He was in his uniform but he was clean and dry, which was impossible. And when did he climb the hill anyway? Where did he come from? Because five seconds ago he wasn't standing there. I was sure of it.

"Move, Tedi," he said again. This time he knelt down next to me and took the knife from my now bleeding hands. "I've got this."

He did? Really? Because things were looking pretty grim at the moment.

Before I could make my swollen and numb lips form words, Jack had taken the knife and swiftly cut across his palm, the blood swelling to the surface immediately. He held his hand over the middle of the circle and a few drops fell to the ground.

Then it all stopped. Everything.

The wind, rain, frogs, snakes. The earth went still and the stones making up the pentagram rolled into a neat stack. The sun was out, the chill was back in the air, and when I looked down at my hands…they were fine. No blisters. No cuts. No swelling. I reached up to touch my face and it felt normal as well. It had all gone back to the way it was before we'd started climbing the hill.

Jack's blood had worked. He was a truly good person. I might have doubted it every now and then but I couldn't argue the results. He'd closed the portal.

We'd done it. The entrance to Hell was closed. Sure, there were many others, but at least Ravenmist wouldn't be the appetizers on a humankind buffet for the dead.

I sat on the grass to catch my breath, breathing in and out slowly until my heart wasn't in my throat anymore, and my stomach didn't feel like it was going to empty its contents.

"What were you doing here?"

Jack's growled query seemed to come out of nowhere. I'd almost forgotten he was right next to me.

"I could ask you the same question."

Reaching out, I grabbed his wrist and turned his hand so I could see his palm. Nothing. Like he'd never sliced it open.

"I guess it's about time for us to have a talk, Tedi."

Yes. I had so many questions. How did he know we were here? How did he climb the hill? How did he know to drop blood in the middle of the pentagram? Was he the one shielding me from the frogs and snakes? And if so...*what in the heck?*

"Let's talk, Jack."

I wanted some answers.

Chapter Fifteen

JACK BUNDLED MISSY and I into his truck and drove toward her home. We hadn't said much. He'd asked her if she was okay and she'd assured him that she was. He hadn't asked me, but then I figured it was obvious that I was fine.

Other than being completely and totally confused. Baffled, really. The entire day had blown my mind and I could barely put together coherent thoughts.

When we arrived at Missy's, she grabbed her bag and then gave me a big hug, a few tears leaking from her eyes.

"We did it," she whispered, a big smile on her face. "We closed it."

"With a little help," I said softly, although I had a feeling that Jack could hear.

Missy glanced at him and then back at me.

"I'm betting you're going to get a full explanation. Call me tomorrow and tell me all about it."

She thanked Jack again, and to my surprise they hugged briefly as well before she turned and entered her home. A light came on in the window and that's when Jack backed out of her driveway and onto the road.

Was Missy right? Was I going to get a full explanation?

Neither of us said anything but I could tell where he was going. He pulled up into the driveway of his condo and came over to my side to open my door. I hopped down and followed him into the house, looking for Tyler.

"He's at a friend's house working on a project for chemistry class," Jack said, reading my mind. "I'll pick him up in about an hour or so."

He shrugged off his coat and draped it over a kitchen chair before starting a pot of coffee. It looked like we weren't going anywhere for awhile, so I shed my coat as well.

"Go on and have a seat in the living room. I'll bring it out when it's done."

I didn't want to argue and I didn't have anything better to do, so I perched on the edge of a sofa cushion. The living room didn't look much different than the last time I'd been there, which was months ago. There wasn't much personality in the decorating. It was still all beige. The only difference today was that it was slightly untidy, with several file folders on the coffee table along with a laptop.

And the diaries. *The diaries.*

"You stole them. Why would you steal them?"

It didn't make a lick of sense. Why would Jack steal the diaries? He didn't care about the history of Ravenmist or what they'd been valued at.

"Did you steal them to protect them or something?"

It didn't make a ton of sense but it might explain the behavior.

"I didn't steal the diaries. I just recovered them today."

Oh.

"Have you told the town?"

"Not yet. I will. I want to show you something, Tedi."

"I have questions, Jack."

"And I'll answer all of them. But first, I want you to watch this."

Jack placed a steaming mug of coffee in front of me before flipping open the laptop and turning the screen so it was facing me.

"Okay, what is it?"

"Just watch."

This. This impatience was familiar. The lack of explanation or details. That was classic Jack, though. It was comforting in a weird way, even though I knew that Jack was more than your everyday sheriff.

He'd known what to do.

The video started, and at first I didn't know what I was watching. The lighting wasn't terrific but I could see an alleyway and a car parked in it. Then a woman came out of a doorway with her hands full of books and walked to the back of the vehicle.

Oh my stars. It was Natalie Martin.

And that alleyway ran in back of the civic center.

A quick check of the timestamp in the corner of the video

told the tale. This was taken from the night of the play and tree-lighting ceremony.

"It was Natalie. Natalie Martin stole the diaries."

Sitting next to me, Jack shook his head. "Watch. It's not over."

Natalie didn't load the books into her car as I'd expected. She looked back over her shoulder and almost directly into the camera. Her eyes were lit up, a glowing red, but it was only for a second. Then she stood there for a long moment before smoke billowed out of her nose and mouth. Leaning closer to the display, I watched mesmerized as a man seemingly appeared out of nowhere from that smokescreen.

Elijah Smith.

Natalie handed him the diaries and he again disappeared into a cloud of smoke while she went back into the civic center. The video was still and then it came to a stop. I wasn't even sure where to begin with all of my questions. I wasn't sure if I could believe my own eyes.

"Could I see that again?"

It was almost surreal. I sounded totally normal but inside I was twisted into knots. Jack cued up the video again and I watched once more. Nothing changed. I still saw what I saw. Clearly, he had watched this before me.

My gaze shifted from the laptop screen to his face. He was obviously waiting for me to speak, as normally he had plenty to say. He would have to pick this moment to be quiet after all this time.

Finally, I pointed to the screen. "I thought your friend couldn't fix the video?"

"I never sent him the video. It was fine from the beginning. I only said that to protect Natalie Martin. Once I saw it I knew that I needed to find a way to bring the investigation to a logical halt. No one else needed to see this. They'd get the wrong idea."

Okay, Jack. What's the *right* idea? How about a hint?

"That man…that was Elijah. I had dinner with him last night."

It wasn't the most obvious place to start but it something.

Jack nodded. "His name isn't Elijah Smith, but yes, that's the same man from the restaurant last night."

"He's…a thief?"

His lips twisted and then he sort of chuckled. "Tedi, that's the least of what he is. I'm not sure where to even start with all of this. There's so much I need to tell you."

"I want to hear it all."

He stood and walked over to the front window. It was dark outside, of course, and the neighborhood was quiet. There wasn't much to see out there but he stared for a few minutes apparently, gathering his thoughts. I kept silent, although it wasn't easy. There were so many questions it almost made my head explode. I hadn't been this confused since I'd learned that Missy was a Grim Reaper.

"I didn't want to drag you into any of this," he began, his back still to me. "I wanted to keep you safe. But when I found out that you were casting a spell to try and find out who the demon was in Ravenmist…well…I knew you were already more than knee-deep in all of this. The fact is, I'm not sure what you know and what you don't know."

Uh….Houston? We have a problem. Because I think I just heard Jack Garrett, a disbeliever in anything supernatural, talk about demons as if he was discussing the weather.

And hold the phone, Virginia. How did he know that we were casting a spell?

I was beginning to feel faint. And a little sick to my stomach.

"How did you know we were trying to cast a spell?"

He turned to look at me and a corner of his mouth was lifted in a wry smile.

"Because I could feel it."

The room spun and I grabbed the coffee cup but then thought better of it, slapping it back down on the table. I kept replaying his words over and over in my head and what they were making me think was so far out of the realm of possibilities… I just couldn't wrap my brain around it.

"I think I might need something stronger than coffee."

And a bunch of it.

Jack rummaged in a cabinet in the kitchen and pulled down a bottle of whiskey and two highball glasses. Pouring out a splash for each of us, he handed me the glass.

"Shall we drink to the truth, Tedi? I guess it's about time."

My hands were literally shaking, but somehow I managed to clink glasses and then drink the shot. It was warm and fiery in my belly but it didn't change the maelstrom in my head.

"What's the truth, Jack?"

He sat down beside me again. "C'mon, Tedi. You're one of the smartest people I know. You know the truth. At least part of it, and I'll tell you the rest."

The truth. The truth. Could it be?

"You're the demon."

There. I'd said it out loud. Disturbingly, nothing happened. There were no fireworks or earthquakes. It was just me and Jack sitting on his beige couch in his beige living room in his beige house.

"I am."

I looked up into his eyes, my gaze searching for something that I could say *Yes, right there. Now it's obvious. I should have known.*

But he looked like everyday, pain in my backside Jack.

"Good…or evil?"

Chuckling, he took my glass and placed it back on the table alongside his, refilling them one more time.

"If I were evil I probably wouldn't tell you the truth, but I am a good demon. I was able to close the portal, after all. I'm here to help, Tedi."

No, he didn't understand.

"Help? You've brought a possible apocalypse to Ravenmist, Jack. That's not helping. All the energy that you have has the ghosts practically living lives again. Evil is coming to fight you and all of humankind could perish. That's not helping."

I needed that second drink. I slung it down quickly, letting it burn its way to my churning stomach. With my luck, it was all going to come back up.

"The apocalypse was going to happen with or without me. I came here to stop it. Tonight when we closed the portal, that's just the battle. Not the war."

"I guess that's good news."

"How long have you known?"

"About you being a demon? I'd say five minutes. If you mean about the impending doom of Ravenmist then I would say last spring. Daisy, Missy, and my mom know, too." Then a thought occurred to me. "Missy is the Grim Reaper."

He nodded. "I figured that out eventually, but I think you should know that Daisy isn't psychic. Not at all."

"Are you sure? Because she told me not to go out last night, and that she had a bad feeling about it and boy, was she right. I should have stayed home."

"Nothing bad was going to happen to you. I was watching the entire time."

My brain had officially exploded into a million gross little pieces. It would start oozing out of my ears any moment. I picked up the highball glass but it was empty. Jack took it from my unresisting fingers and placed it out of my reach.

"I don't think you should have another."

"Even if I need it?"

"You don't need it. You've got this." He scratched his chin. "You never suspected? Really? There were so many times I thought you'd guessed. Especially that night when I caught you and Missy at Ravenmist Lake. I assume you were there to speak to some souls that hadn't passed on? I didn't put it all together until later, I have to admit."

"The Young Lovers. They live with Daisy now."

"They had a nice wedding," he agreed. "Isn't it strange how no one figured out they were spirits? It's almost like the entire town decided that they were alive and human and everyone is going with it. A group delusion. I've seen it happen before."

"How long have you known? About the Young Lovers?"

"From the moment I saw them at the diner."

"And Terrence? You saw him too, but you never said anything."

"Who's Terrence?"

"The ghost you saw in my office."

"Right. I didn't know his name. No, I didn't say anything."

I was actually starting to get mad, which was an improvement over sick to my stomach.

"All this time you've pretended not to believe but you really did? You made fun of us, Jack. And your own son, too. That's not nice."

He held up his hands in a sign of surrender. "Now hold on a minute. I never made fun of anyone, least of all Tyler. I told him that I didn't believe and needed evidence, which I think is a good thing to teach a young man. Solid evidence is important."

"But you're a demon." Another thought occurred to me. My brain might just be functioning again. "Wait…is Tyler a demon, too?"

"Yes, but he doesn't know it. Neither did I until I was an adult."

Pressing my palm to my forehead, I groaned softly. "My head hurts."

"I'm sure it does. Perhaps I should start from the beginning?"

"The beginning? That sounds like a plan. I'll let you do the talking for a little while."

While I silently and slowly went out of my mind.

Chapter Sixteen

SETTLING BACK ON the couch cushion, I waited for Jack to begin his story. In a way, it was almost like an out of body experience. I was standing outside myself looking on while Jack paced the small living room and tried to articulate what I could barely comprehend.

"I didn't know I was a demon growing up," he began, leaning against the mantle of the small fireplace. "My parents had passed on when I was young. I was told it was a car accident but I later learned that wasn't the case. They were killed by a group of evil demons. One of them was the demon you had dinner with last night."

Whoa. I'd had dinner with a demon?

"Elijah is an evil demon?"

"He is, although as I said before that's not his real name."

"What is his real name?"

Dumb question. Did it really matter?

"I don't know. I've heard him referred to by a few names. Orien is the main one, which is Greek for the hunter. He's an old demon, probably close to a thousand years in age."

"And he killed your parents?"

Jack nodded. "For their power, of course. They were both demons and Orien was trying to steal their energy. It went awry, however, when a friend arrived and kept Orien from doing the ceremony to steal the power. As their son, both of their powers automatically came to me, plus what I was born with."

"So you're like...three demons?"

"Something like that. If I don't have any more children, Tyler will eventually inherit my power and he'll be like four."

"But you didn't know you were a demon? And Tyler doesn't know, either?"

"Yes, and it's not unusual. I wasn't told until I was nineteen when my power started coming in. I'll tell Tyler before then so he has a little more warning than I had."

"And your wife...?"

Another stupid question.

"Ex-wife," he corrected. "She was not a demon, but she knew. I told her once we were married. She's taken the vow of secrecy. I have many issues with Lacey but I know she'll take that secret to her grave."

Lacey. Her name was Lacey. I'd learned more than I bargained for tonight. And she'd taken a vow of secrecy too, so she had to be a pretty decent human being. This wouldn't be an easy secret to keep.

Then I realized that I was going to have to keep this secret, at least from people outside my inner circle.

"But you and Tyler are good demons?"

"Yes, there aren't a lot of us." He frowned. "I guess I should tell you why I'm here."

"That would be nice."

"Tedi, you're being too polite. It's not like you. Scream and yell at me or something. You're far too pale."

"That's because I'm really unconscious or dead and I'll wake up and this will all be a weird dream because I ate spicy food."

"I wish that were the case. More than you know. I can get you some fresh coffee."

"No, thank you. I'm just going to let you talk."

"I know that you're not yourself when you've turned down coffee." He rubbed the back of his neck. "Why don't we change tactics here? Why don't you tell me what you already know?"

Since I didn't know much that was easy.

"That the battle between good and evil has been going on since the dawn of the universe," I recited, remembering the information that Missy had found. "Good and evil were created equal and they have been trying to steal power back and forth for centuries. Because there are less good demons than bad, supposedly the good demons have more power per demon. At least that's what we were counting on when we realized the supernatural energy surge was probably from a demon moving into Ravenmist."

"And since very few people move into town," Jack said. "You had to know that I was on the list of possibles."

I looked up at him, not bothering to hide the truth. "Never in a million years did I think it was you. You were so dismissive of the supernatural in general. I'd have thought it was the Carmodys rather than you."

Jack seemed amused at that and couldn't hide his mirth.

"That's what I intended for you to think. It's what I intended for everyone in town to think."

"So you lied to all of us."

"Because I had to."

That's wasn't what this really about, though. Hopping up from the couch, I walked right up to him and poked him in the chest with my finger.

"You lied to *me*, Jack. Me. I thought we were friends. You don't lie to your friends."

The last part was said with a sob and the next thing I knew I was crying. I hate that. I hate showing weakness in front of anyone, and most of all Jack.

"I've been lying to people my entire life so I'm used to it. But I have to say, Tedi, that I didn't enjoy lying to you."

He tried to reach out to me then but I brushed away his hand. I was too angry to be mollified, and I wanted to feel that anger. I wanted to nurture it if only for a little while.

"You did it anyway."

He sighed heavily. "Yes, I did it anyway. So what else do you know?"

I shrugged. "Not much more. We were trying to find out who the demon was with the spell, which it appears is how you found out that I knew. Missy's grandmother warned us that the demon would know but we thought it would be worth it. We wanted to identify the demon and then hope to cast some sort of spell to stop him. Or her."

"What you did was dangerous," Jack growled. "And now Orien knows that you know. He felt that spell just as much as I did."

The reality of what we'd taken on was beginning to sink in.

"Was he planning to kill me last night?"

"No, asking you to dinner was just him playing a game with me. He never intended to hurt you as far as I can tell. He wanted to hurt me."

"How could going out to dinner with me hurt you?"

Jack rarely smiled but when he did, he was quite...attractive.

"Ah Tedi, you have to know by now."

No, I didn't know.

"You turned me down–"

"Because I was trying to protect you. Anyone that I'm close to is a target. Of course, now I know that you've been wading in it for months."

"You asked me out–"

"And then left for Chicago. There was a problem there with some evil demons that I had to help with. When I came back, I decided not to ask you out again because I didn't want you to get hurt."

He'd been trying to protect me these last months? Interesting.

"You've been a jerk to everyone since you came back. Really grouchy."

"That's true, but in my defense, I've been trying to stop the slaughter of mankind, so maybe you could cut me some slack?"

He had a valid point. It seemed like we had come full circle since the beginning of this conversation.

"What have you been doing and why did the evil guy want the diaries?"

"I've been trying to find the entrance to Hell so that I can seal it. My belief is that Orien stole the diaries because they may contain a code that points to the location."

"So there's no treasure?"

"I think the story has been twisted to be more palatable to the masses. Orien stole the diaries to break the code so he could find the portal to Hell and open it when the time is right."

"What time would that be?" I asked with real fear in my heart. Was it soon?

"When I'm dead and out of the way."

"Oh."

"Not that I'm planning on being that way anytime in the near future, but then neither is he. One of us is wrong."

As much as Jack made me mad, I didn't want him dead. But I still had unanswered questions. So many of them I could barely keep them straight.

"How did you get the diaries back? Did you have to fight Orien?"

Because he'd looked fine at dinner. Did demons heal faster than humans? I needed to add that question to my list.

Jack shook his head. "I found his nest and stole them back.

He's probably just realizing they're gone right about now."

One word jumped out at me.

"Nest?"

"It's a term we use for where a demon feels safe. There are usually spells and charms protecting it."

"You have spells protecting this condo?"

"I do. Tyler, too."

And yet those spells hadn't protected him from having a bad interior design. Beige.

"How did you get past Orien's spells?"

"That's difficult to explain. Sort of how I got past the spells at the portal."

"It doesn't appear that I'm going anywhere soon. I've got loads of time on my hands."

"Fine, I have an…object that belonged to my parents. It has powers that allow me to bypass many – but not all – protection spells. It helped me push back on your spell."

"See? That wasn't so hard." I was on a roll so I figured I should push forward. "What kind of powers do you have anyway?"

I'd always wanted to be able to fly. Or be invisible. That would be cool.

"We live very long lives. We need less sleep but we also need more food." That I could have guessed. Jack could out-eat anyone I'd ever known. It all made sense now. "We're stronger and faster. Our senses are more finely tuned and our brains process information faster. We can also possess other people's bodies. That's what you saw with Natalie Martin. Orien possessed her body and stole the diaries. She, of course, has no memory of what she did, which is all for the best, really. As for other powers, those are standard across the board. Then there are inherited powers or powers given by a sacred object. For example, from my mother I inherited the ability to see through objects. That's how I was able to read your letter to Santa. I had my hand on the mailbox and could see through it and the envelope."

Mind officially blown. *Jack* was my secret Santa?

"You've been the one sending me gifts?"

He shrugged awkwardly. "I felt badly about how I've been acting lately. Did you like the snow?"

Jack was a demon and he also had a conscience. Who woulda thunk it?

"You made it snow? For me?"

I was actually choked up.

"It wasn't Jack Frost, Tedi."

"So you also have power over the weather?"

This just might come in handy. My mind was whirling with plans.

"That's from my dad. In a limited way, I can control the elements. Making snow wasn't easy, by the way. I was exhausted afterward."

But I was worth it. He didn't say it out loud but he could've given up. I wouldn't have known the difference.

"Thank you."

We sort of stared at each other for awhile, neither one of us saying anything. I could still hear the words in my head over and over...

Jack was – is – a demon.

And he *likes* me.

It wasn't the worst thing in the world. In fact, I wasn't complaining at all. Life was looking gosh darn good.

Wait...did Jack say something about this only being the battle and not the war?

"So BOTH YOU and this Orien were looking for the entrance to Hell?"

The question sounded jarring as we'd been quiet for so long, but it was now the number one, most important query I could think of.

"Theoretically. I'd been looking for it since I arrived in town, but I hadn't found it yet. Not until today when I felt your return into town."

"You could tell when I came back to town?"

"Yes, Tedi. I was beside myself when I felt you leaving Ravenmist. I didn't know where you were and when I talked to your mother, she was vague."

I'd tell him about my trip to Hell. Later. I had a distinct feeling that he wasn't going to be happy about my journey.

"You talked to my mom?"

"Yes. I kind of got the feeling she doesn't like me much."

Oh. I'd have to explain that later.

"Don't worry about her. She does like you. Really."

"If you say so."

"So Orien wanted to open the portal?"

"He wants to make it permanently open so that beings from the underworld can pass freely onto our realm. I could not allow that to happen."

"Now that we've closed the entrance, what do we do now?"

"There is no *we* here," he replied firmly, wearing a frown. "This is my responsibility, and it's dangerous. You could get hurt or killed. I'm not about to let that happen."

Having Jack say *no* to me wasn't new so I'd learned to ignore him. This time wasn't going to be any different. He ought to know that by now.

I pointed to myself. "From what you've said, I'm in danger just by existing. All of us, isn't that correct?"

"Yes."

His tone was irritable but that was his charm.

"When it's my patootie on the line, you can bet I'm not going to sit back and wait to die a horrible death from an evil entity. I'm going out fighting, Jack. So will my friends and family. This isn't a *you* problem. This is an *us* problem. We're all in danger so you can forget acting like a one-man army. Now you've got backup."

He leaned down until we were almost nose to nose. "I think that it's admirable that you want to fight the good fight but it's my job – literally – to protect you and this town. Not just as a demon of good but as the sheriff. Your...patootie is safe with me."

We both burst into laughter then at his ridiculously sounding statement, but the unfortunately the laughter didn't last. The situation wasn't funny.

"It's too late," I finally said. "I'm helping. We can do this the easy way, which is you directing that help or I can go behind your back. You choose."

He growled, and honest-to-frog it sounded otherworldly. Like how a demon would sound if he'd growled. Like that. You know what I mean?

"You are the most stubborn, infuriating woman that I have ever met in my entire life. In all that time, you're the most mule-headed."

Jack was such a sweet talker.

And we so needed to talk about just how old he really was. If Orien was about a thousand, what was Jack? I wanted to hear about it all.

"I've always been a bit of an overachiever. You can ask my parents. Now what do we do first? Take the diaries back to the civic center?"

I was revved up and ready to go. We finally had some might in this battle.

With Jack on our side, we'd win this war with evil. Hands down.

Chapter Seventeen

"HEAVENS TO BETSY, Tedi. Jack is the good demon?"

That overwrought voice was from my supposedly best friend in the whole wide world, Missy. We were standing in my living room the next morning – me, Missy, Daisy, and Mom. Jack had placed some sort of charm on the inn to protect it. And me. It involved a tiny gold heart that he'd buried near the front door. I'd felt a burst of cold air and then Jack said it was done. Orien couldn't see into the inn, and if he came within half a mile of it Jack would know.

He'd argued with me again when he dropped me at home. He wasn't sure this was the best idea but I'd convinced him that if he didn't let me help I was going to go off on my own and do it anyway. He'd had that resigned expression on his face and honestly, he'd looked tired as well. I'd tell him about my trip to Hell another time. When he was more rested.

Oh…did I mention that he asked me out on a date? A real one. Nothing was going to get in the way this time. He'd promised.

Look at me, folks. I go from having almost no social life to two dates in the space of a few days. I was something of a vamp. Woohoo.

"He is," I confirmed. "He's here to stop the apocalypse."

Daisy was nodding as if she knew all along.

"There was something different about him," she said. "I just couldn't put my finger on it."

"It explains so much," my mother agreed. "So what happens now?"

"Jack said we would talk about it tonight...on our date."

Pandemonium. They may not have been happy about my date the other night but they were positively giddy about me going out with Jack.

"We'll help you pick out an outfit," my mother said, her hands clasped with glee.

"Maybe you should wear your hair up," Daisy suggested.

"I think you should wear that new lipstick," Missy said. "It will look fabulous on you."

Not a bad idea. I wanted to look good, but deep inside I knew that Jack wasn't the type to care about stuff like that. He'd seen me look pretty awful today and he'd still asked me out.

I had a date. And this time? I was excited about it.

UNLIKE THE OTHER night, I didn't think too long about how I was going to dress for my date with Jack. At this point, he knew me – warts and all – so freaking out about which shade of lipstick to wear was a waste of time. Although I did, indeed, wear the new lipstick he'd bought me for Christmas.

I'd dressed nicely, but comfortably, in black jeans and my new seafoam green sweater. I took a few extra minutes with my makeup to create a smoky eye, but everything else was strictly what I would have worn when going out to dinner with anyone. Knowing Jack, he'd show up in his uniform straight from work.

Oops. Jack showed up at my door looking freshly showered, shaved, and dressed quite nicely in dark wash jeans and a brown sweater.

Holding a freakin' bouquet of flowers. Who knew he was a romance ninja?

"Jack."

"Tedi."

"You brought flowers."

"Are you allergic?"

"No, I'm just surprised."

"Sometimes I surprise even myself." He held them out, still standing in my lobby. Tina at the front desk was gaping like a fish out of water. In less than an hour, Jack and I would be the talk of the town. "Are you going to take them?"

Was I? Yes, I was. Tina flew around the corner of her counter, her gaze still stuck on Jack. "Um, Tedi...I can take those for you and put them in water."

I handed them off like a quarterback at the Super Bowl. "That would be wonderful. Thank you, Tina."

"I was thinking we'd go to the Italian place, but I'm open to anything you might be in the mood for."

"Italian sounds perfect."

We chatted on the way to the restaurant. Mostly about his announcement to the town that he'd recovered the diaries. I thought his explanation was lame but everyone was lapping it up without question. He'd told them that they'd shown up at the sheriff's station in a package postmarked from Chicago. How he'd managed it I didn't know but he'd even had a box with an address label to show the town. Both the Martins and the Farradays had been incredibly grateful and I'd watched as Natalie and Frank actually spoke to one another for the first time in their lives. They were both sure it had been the Cambridges. Strange circumstances had brought them together.

That was it. He didn't go into any more detail, knowing that the people would put their own spin on the story. By tomorrow morning there would be a dozen or more theories as to who took them and why. None of them correct, of course, but as he'd pointed out it was the fun of creating the stories and gossip. Mostly the town was simply glad that the diaries were back.

When we arrived at the restaurant, I could feel all the eyes on us as we were led to our table. I'm not exaggerating here. Literally, everyone was looking at us.

"They're staring," I said unnecessarily. His demon senses had surely picked it up before mine had. "It's like we're animals in a zoo."

"Just ignore them. They'll get used to seeing us together eventually."

I settled into my chair and hid behind my menu. "You're assuming this date is going to go well and that we're going to want to repeat this."

He chuckled and placed his own menu off to the side. "I figure we know the good and the bad by now. I doubt there are too many surprises ahead."

Looking over the top of my menu, I rolled my eyes. "Are you kidding me? You're a supernatural being. I have questions. Lots of them."

"I'm an open book."

"That's a laugh. You've never been an open book, Jack Garrett."

"You've caught me in a good mood. We closed the portal, Tedi. Let's celebrate."

I wanted to but...

"You said this was only the battle, not the war."

"That's true," he conceded. "But we celebrate when we can. We won't win every time."

"I don't like the sound of that."

"I don't like it either, but it's the reality."

"Seriously, what do we do next?"

"We prepare. Orien might be defeated but he'll be back. Not if, but when. He'll regroup and come back with another plan. We have to be ready."

"I'm listening. How do we do that?"

Jack stroked his chin. "We might want to think about finding a sacred object that's powerful enough to either protect the town or defeat Orien."

"Okay, let's do that."

"Whoa," he said with a smile, holding his hands up in surrender. "It's not that easy. First, we need to research what those objects might be and then find them. If it were simple, anyone could do it."

"Now you have help."

"Yes, I do. Now what are you going to order for dinner, Tedi? I think I'm going to have the chicken parmesan."

We were finishing up our dinner when Iris Martin and Elliott Farraday walked into the restaurant. Together.

Now no one was looking at Jack and I. They were staring at Iris and Elliott. Clearly, the two were smitten with one another. They were giving each other goo-goo eyes and holding hands.

"Why do you look so shocked?" Jack asked, his gaze following mine to the happy couple. "Wasn't that on your Christmas list? You wanted the two families to be reunited?"

I looked back at the man across the table from me in surprise. "Jack Garrett, did you play demon matchmaker?"

"It didn't take much. They obviously liked each other. I just gave them some encouragement when I talked to them about the diaries. They did the rest."

"I never realized you were such a romantic." I peered up at him from under my lashes. "And thank you. I've never gotten so many Christmas wishes granted before."

"You're welcome. I'm still hungry for dessert. How about we order some?"

Some things never changed and that was comforting. We shared a huge slab of apple pie with a scoop of ice cream on top. When I say shared, I mean he had seventy-five percent of it but he had stopped an evil demon from opening a portal to Hell.

Hey, maybe this was why I was having so much trouble being an optimist. Ravenmist was the backyard to Hades.

And I was its innkeeper.

Later when Jack dropped me at home we kissed, and it was everything I was hoping it would be and more. I think he might have been using some demon mojo because when his lips touched mine, I swear I saw fireworks. But that was Jack. Over the top and not in the least ordinary.

The kiss was a heck of way to top off an amazing day. What a way to kick off a magical Christmas season...

Christmas Eve...

IT WAS ALMOST midnight at Jack's condo. The tree in the corner glittered like diamonds with its gold and silver ornaments. I'd done the best I could with the beige decor and added several bright red poinsettias around the house and on the mantle.

Jack and I had exchanged gifts after Tyler went to bed and then toasted in the holiday with some champagne. He'd liked the vintage rock music albums and the navy sweater I'd purchased for him, and needless to say, I'd loved the new *Little House* and *Harry Potter* books that he'd gifted me.

There were shiny bows and wrapping paper on the floor where we'd discarded them and I really should have cleaned it all up. But I was happily sipping at my champagne and enjoying the sizzle and pop of the logs in the fireplace, zoning out and staring at the leaping orange and yellow flames. Jack had excused himself to check on Tyler and I'd tucked my socked feet under me on the couch cushion and sat back after a long and busy day.

We had another one ahead of us tomorrow. Dinner and presents with my parents, plus Daisy, Missy, and her boyfriend Dylan. Oops, scratch that. I'd received a text a few minutes ago from Missy that Dylan had proposed. He was her fiancé now. I couldn't imagine two people more meant for each other.

As for me and Jack...

We'd fallen easily into a relationship since that first date. There hadn't been any handwringing or drama – unless you counted closing the portal. It felt so normal and natural. It was as if this was what was supposed to happen. Jack could still be grumpy and I could still be high strung, but for the most part we were fine with it.

There was another loud pop from the fireplace that snagged my attention and then it morphed in front of my eyes, growing wide and taller until a rotund man in a red suit stepped out of it.

Oh my stars. It was Santa Claus.

His red hat with white fur sat jauntily on his head and just like in the stories, there was a little bit of cinder dust on the trim of his jacket. His blue eyes twinkled merrily and his smile was wide in his round cheeks. He gave me a wink and then set immediately to work, pulling brightly colored packages from his oversized bag.

"Santa?"

He turned when I said his name, placing one last gift under the sparkling tree.

"Merry Christmas, Tedi. Has it been a good one so far?"

Feeling dizzy, I had to force the words out of my mouth. I was talking to *the* Santa Claus.

"It has, thank you. I hope you're having a lovely holiday season as well."

My mother would have been proud of how polite I was being. Not screaming and all.

"We are, and thank you for asking about the missus, the elves, and the reindeer. They're doing fine, too." He stood then, taller than I'd pictured in my mind. He was an elf, right? "You've been a good girl this year, Tedi. Keep it up and you might get that pony."

I didn't get a chance to reply. As quick as he'd shown up, he was gone and everything had gone back to the way it was. Had it even really happened? Perhaps I'd had a little too much champagne?

I looked down at the base of the tree I'd helped Jack decorate and yes, there were more gifts there. I crawled down from the couch and reached out to touch them.

They were real.

"What are you doing?"

"They're real."

Jack was looking at me strangely but that wasn't all that unusual. He had that look a lot these days.

"Did you think they weren't? Did Santa drop them off?"

I nodded. "He was just here. He told me I'd been good this year."

"He doesn't spend that much time with you and it shows." Jack reached down to the coffee table and lifted up an empty glass. He and Tyler had laughingly left out a plate of cookies and a glass of eggnog for Santa. The plate was now empty and so was the glass.

When…? It had all been a blur.

"My life is very strange, Jack."

"You don't sound upset about it."

I wasn't. I wouldn't trade it for the world.

"I'm not. How about some more champagne?"

Jack was right. We might as well celebrate the small victories. This was the calm before the storm and we'd better enjoy it while we could.

A little peace on earth never hurt anyone. We'd earned it.

I hope you enjoyed Grandma Got Run Over By A Demon! There will be more in the Ravenmist Whodunit series coming soon.
Thank you for reading.

About The Author

Olivia Jaymes is a wife, mother, lover of sexy romance and cozy mysteries, and caffeine addict. She lives with her husband, son, and two spoiled dogs in central Florida and spends her days typing on her computer with a canine on her lap.

She is currently working on a new cozy mystery series – *A Ravenmist Whodunit* – in addition to her other ongoing romance series.

Visit Olivia Jaymes at
www.OliviaJaymes.com

www.ingramcontent.com/pod-product-compliance
Lightning Source LLC
Chambersburg PA
CBHW050848180626
46814CB00007B/2671